D1826445

Good Intentions
The Dead War Series

D.N. Simmons

First Edition

RUSHMORE PUBLISHING

First Edition Edited by H.I. Gantt
Copyright © 2013 by D.N. Simmons
Rushmore Publishing - Chicago, IL
ISBN-13: 978-0615887524
ISBN-10: 061588752X

Dedication

I would like to dedicate this novel to my absolutely wonderful, loyal, understanding and *truly* patient readership. Your unwavering support has meant the world to me. Writing these books for you has been one of my greatest pleasures and I am thrilled to have you all as readers.

As always, I would also like to thank my editor H.I. Gantt, for being honest and so very supportive. I love you.

I'd like to thank my mother for being the wonderful, supportive and loving person you are, honestly, I wouldn't be here without you. I'd like to thank my father (may he forever rest in peace) for his encouragement, sense of humor and advice given, that has guided me on my life's journey.

Last, but not least, I'd like to send a special "thank you" to all of you who have supported me in life and in my career.

Love Always
D.N.

And So It Begins...

Prologue

The Director of the Biological Research Department of SciTech Laboratories, Dr. Steve Morris sat at his desk in his comfortable black, leather chair as he spoke with the military general across from him.

"I'm sure I don't have to tell you that this little experiment is to be kept top secret?" General Bradley Fuller reiterated. His cold blue eyes attempted to cut ribbons through the debonair attitude of the younger man.

Dr. Morris cleared his throat, blatantly ignoring the General's glare. "I understand full well the importance of secrecy in this matter and I can assure you that you have nothing to worry about."

"If it's all the same to you, I'll be the judge of that. Trusting SciTech Labs with this wasn't my choice. However, this company came highly recommended as one of the top labs in the entire country, so here I am." The General crossed one leg over the other as he rested his hands on his knee. "What can you guarantee as the turnaround time? We want results as soon as possible."

"Well, from what you've shown me, it's an unknown substance. It might help us if you can give me a little more background on the compound. It would help us to know where it came from," Steve said.

The General frowned. "Unfortunately, that's classified."

Steve scoffed. "General, you've got my hands tied—"

"It's need to know and you don't have the clearance," Gen. Fuller interjected brashly. "If you don't think your department can work under those circumstances I'll inform my superiors of your noncompliance."

"General, please, there's no need for rashness. I only want to give the United States Military Forces our very best effort."

"The United States Military isn't looking for 'effort', Doctor. We're looking for results and with what you're being offered to come up with those results, failure is not an option. Are we clear?"

Gen. Fuller's stern gaze became even more intense. The nerves Steve was trying to ignore came roaring to the forefront. He shifted in his chair, feeling a lot less comfortable.

Steve cleared his throat. "As they say in the military, crystal."

Steve adjusted the knot of his tie, loosening the material a bit. The room was feeling a bit hotter than it was several minutes ago before the general entered. He couldn't help but wonder if it was because the heat was turned up or if it was just him.

"I'd like to meet the team you're going to assign to this experiment," Gen. Fuller requested.

"Oh, of course. One minute." Steven pressed several buttons on his phone keypad and a masculine voice came over the intercom.

"Yes, Dr. Morris?" Dr. Vincent Masterson replied.

"I'd like you to gather your team and come to my office," Steve ordered.

"We'll be there shortly."

The line disconnected. The two men sitting in the office looked at each other for a few seconds before Gen. Fuller broke the uncomfortable silence. "You still didn't give me a turnaround time."

"You'll have to forgive me General, but with so little information provided to us regarding this compound, I can't in good conscious give you an exact date," Steve said.

"You have six months."

"Six months? I think it's premature to attempt to put a time limit on this project."

"Regardless of your opinion, six months is the limit. We would prefer results before that date, of course. You'll have every resource you'll need at your disposal. If after six months, you come to me empty handed, you will lose the sizable grant your company is being awarded based on your success with this project."

Steve thought about the huge amount of money the military was tossing at them and the threat struck home. His superiors put a lot of pressure on him to get the job done. They didn't care how he did it, they just wanted it done. When he'd first been approached about the secret military project, he was intrigued, but cautious. Knowing that the success of the experiment was up to him, he made sure to gather three of his best scientists for the job. Transferring the pressure and duties of jobs was something he was well versed at. His telephone rang and his secretary informed him that his team had arrived and was standing outside the door.

"Please let them in," Steve said before hanging up.

"Hi, Steve, you wanted to see us?" Vincent greeted as he entered.

"Yes, please." He gestured around the room, indicating that the three scientists should find a place in the room to either stand or sit.

Vincent took the chair beside the General's and his other co-workers—Dr. Henrick and Dr. Pierce—stood behind him.

"This is General Fuller, he's our military contact on the project I've informed you about." Steve said before giving full but brief introductions.

Gen. Fuller gave the three men a quick inspection. They were younger than he had expected. The one called Vincent in particular—with his freshly shaven face, bright blue eyes and carefree, but rather preppy haircut. His eyes trailed over to Dr. Henrick, who looked to be a little older with chestnut hair and brown eyes. Then there was dark haired, brown eyed Dr. Philip who looked to be fresh out of med school, as far as he was concerned. Looking at the team of scientist, his hopes for success were abysmally low.

"It's nice to meet you, General. I hope you're enjoying our Chicago weather," Vincent said in an attempt to make light conversation.

"I've been in worst conditions." was the General's curt reply.

Vincent took the hint and decided to keep the conversation to strictly business.

"The good General just wanted to meet our top-notch team who will be heading the experiment. I assure you, Gen. Fuller, these three men are our best and if results are what you're looking for, they will be the scientists who will give them to you," Steve boasted.

Vincent cut a glance at Steve wondering just how much shit he was getting them in to.

"Are you up to the task?" Gen. Fuller asked the scientists.

"Not only am I up to the task, I'm very intrigued by it. We've already started the preliminary tests and I can't begin to tell you how fascinating this substance is," Vincent asked, leaning forward in his excitement. "May I ask where you got it?"

Steve coughed and when Vincent turned to him, he gave a slight shake of his head.

"I'm sorry, Doctor, but that information, as I explained to your superior, is classified." Gen. Fuller left it at that, keeping his face as stoic as any trained soldier could and giving new defining meaning to a "killer poker face".

Vincent nodded with a crocked smile. "Yes, of course, I understand."

"If you don't have anything else to discuss with these scientists, why don't we let them get back to work. Time is of the essence, is it not?" Steve said.

He tried very hard to conceal the sarcasm he wanted to douse the uptight military general with, but out of respect—and fear—he held it in check.

General Fuller nodded as he picked up his hat from the desktop, placing it back on his bald head. He rose from his chair. "You're quite right. I need to be leaving. I have a plane to catch in an hour. We're trusting SciTech Labs and your team with something that will change the world as we know it. You are all going to be a huge part of history, mark my words."

"We hope so, General," Steve said as he rose from his seat to escort the general out of the building.

Vincent and the other doctors took the lead and left the office first, returning to their laboratory. Steve couldn't help basking in the relief he felt as he watched the general climb into the back of a military Hummer.

"Fucking asshole," he muttered to himself as he turned to go back to his office. Once inside, he contacted Vincent and asked him to come back to his office alone.

Several minutes later, Vincent knocked on the door. Steven opened it and stepped aside.

"Is there something wrong?" Vincent asked as he entered. He tried not to sound as nervous as he felt.

"Only that you can't fail. Not with this. We have millions riding on the success of this project. I promoted you and gave you your own lab and team because you guaranteed me that you were the man for the job. Now, I ask you, can you do it?" Steve looked at him, searching Vincent's expression for any signs of doubt.

"First off, Steve, you promoted me because *you* told me I was the best scientist for the job. We've just started the project, but it would be a lot easier if we knew more about what we're working with. Do you have any information about the origins of this compound we're supposed to revolutionize?" Vincent asked with a bit of unprofessional sarcasm, not entirely uncharacteristic of him.

Steve sighed. "I don't know anything more than you do. When I pressed him for answers, I got the same response he gave you." He ran his hands over his face, then back through his blond locks. "This is big, Vincent. He was right when he said it would change the world. Do you think we'll be successful?"

By we, you mean us. Vincent thought, knowing full well the weight of this project was resting on his shoulders and his team. Although, mainly him because he was in charge of the lab.

"I think we're your best chance. We're just going to need some time."

"You have six months max."

"Well, that's not adding any pressure," Vincent quipped.

"That's the military for you."

"Well, let me get back to work then."

"Go make history."

Vincent nodded and walked out of the room for the second time that day with a since of dread and excitement. "Time to change the world," he said to himself while riding the elevator to the sixth floor.

Chapter One
Five Months and Three Weeks Later

"So this is your current analysis?"

Dr. Vincent Masterson's supervisor, Dr. Steve Morris, spoke as he sifted through the file he was given. The results were unsatisfactory in the least of opinions, and his work was typically some of the best. Subpar was not an option.

"Unfortunately, yes. We ran tests on several different subjects. At best, the results with specimen 12-19 were inconclusive," Vincent said. "The other specimens were unchanged apart from healing their sickness, or minor self-inflicted injuries."

"What happened with specimen 12-19?"

"He suffered a cardiac arrest for about three minutes, but we managed to resuscitate him. The test results didn't show any change in his physical abilities. However, his heart rate is abnormal. Also his health seems to be deteriorating regardless of how much VH-12 we give him," Vincent said.

"Dr. Masterson, I hope I don't have to stress just how important this project is. If we can manipulate the compound, the possibilities in its use can be endless. And let's not forget the massive amount of funding the lab is getting to conduct these tests. The government wants results and we have less than a week to give them to them," Steve reminded him.

"I'm well aware of what's at stake here, sir. But you have to understand that we are working with a very volatile substance. By itself, it's been proven to be highly addictive and even lethal. On the other hand, it can cure every disease known to man. It's even been able to heal broken bones and major injuries in a matter of seconds," Vincent said. "But what we're doing with it... trying to bio-engineer something this unknown... it's going to take time."

"Time we don't have. We have to present something to the board and the military advisers by next week. Have something worthwhile to show by next Wednesday, Mr. Masterson," Steve said.

Vincent didn't need to hear the words "or else" to know they were implied nonetheless. He nodded and left the supervisor's office heading straight into the employee lunch room towards the coffee machine to pour himself a large cup—black.

"I can tell by the lack of cream and sugar in the coffee, your meeting with Morris didn't go well?" Dr. Richard Benton said, patting Vincent on his back.

"Do they ever? The guy's a fucking bureaucrat. He may have been a scientist a long time ago, but now he's just a money-hungry parasite," Vincent said.

"Wow, tell me how you *really* feel about the SOB," Richard said with a chuckle.

Vincent laughed without really wanting to. He wanted to be pissed, but Richard's sense of humor always rubbed off on him at the most inconvenient of times. Still, he was grateful for his friend's timely sense of humor. Already he could feel some of his stress fading away, though he suspected it would return as soon as he walked back into his lab.

"Listen, my wife and I are having a little get together at my house Saturday. Why don't you bring Sarah over? You look like you could use the break and there's going to be beer, ribs, beer, more food, beer and music. Did I mention we're having beer and other liquors that could get you nice and shitfaced?" Richard smiled mischievously as he wiggled his eyebrows.

"You're going to have beer there, you say?" Vincent asked sarcastically.

Richard shrugged. "Just a few bottles. Nothing special." He grinned.

Vincent laughed outright, slapping his friend on the arm. "Yeah, yeah, that sounds good. I could use the distraction."

"Good, cause I've already told Linda you're coming," Richard said, smiling wider.

"Oh you did, did you?" Vincent shook his head as he slipped his dollar into the vending machine. "Man, you're something else."

He pressed the buttons and a Snickers candy bar fell to the bottom. Vincent retrieved it and both he and Richard sat down at the table to enjoy their snacks and coffee. They chatted idly about the current weather, sports and other co-workers for a while.

"So, do you think you're close to discovering the first super-human elixir?" Richard asked him, bringing the conversation to Vincent's supposedly "secret" project.

"How in the hell do *you* know about what we're working on?" Vincent asked, shocked.

Richard cocked an eyebrow as if to say "really?" then shrugged. "Apparently, Morris has a big mouth, especially when he's pillow talking Cathy."

Vincent's eyebrows shot up and he leaned forward. "Wait, Steve Morris and Cathy Billroy are fucking?"

Richard snorted. "Where the hell have you been, man? I thought the whole company new about that. Cathy's been walking around bragging that he's going to leave his wife for her. Frankly, I don't see that happening. His wife has all the money in the family. He's stupid for cheating on her with a big-mouth gossip like Cathy, but I guess she's got that kind of snatch that makes a man do some stupid shit."

"You kiss your wife with that vulgar mouth of yours?" Vincent teased.

"If you knew the things I do with my mouth to that woman—"

Vincent held up his hand. "I'm going to stop you right there on the grounds of too much fucking information." He laughed.

Richard winked. "I'm just saying."

"Yeah, back to what you were saying earlier... about my project..." Vincent sighed and leaned back into his chair. "Truth be told, it's not looking good. That's what the meeting was about. I think our only test subject that had some semblance of success is going to pass away. So I feel like we're taking two steps back. There are some things I haven't tried, but I don't think they're the best options."

"Who knows," Richard stuck another potato chip into his mouth, "the shit you haven't tried might just be the one thing you need to try."

Vincent regarded him thoughtfully. "You might be right. I'll run some other tests before I try those other two options. Just to make sure I'm dotting all my *I's* and crossing all of my *T's*."

"Do what you have to do." Richard looked down at his watch. "Listen, my break is over. I'll see you this Saturday, right?" He pointed at him as he rose from his chair.

Vincent nodded. "Yeah, Sarah and I will be there at about two, is that cool?"

"Perfect, see you then." Richard walked toward the door making sure to toss his trash in the waste paper basket on the way out.

Vincent sipped the last drop of his bitter coffee and rose from the table. He tossed the Styrofoam cup in the recycling bin and went straight to his lab. After donning the bio-protective suit, he went through the decontamination chamber and stood still under the chemical mist. Once the process was complete, he walked out of the chamber into the lab and met up with his fellow scientists.

"How is test subject 12-19?" Vincent asked in greeting.

"There has been a steady decline in his health. I administered six milliliters of the VH-32 into the solution in 12-19's IV, but there's been no change as of yet," Dr. Philip Pierce informed.

Vincent sighed again. In spite of some very violent and undesired side effects, VH-32 was the most concentrated formula they had. It was able to heal broken bones and cure full blown AIDS in less than sixty-seconds. Unfortunately, the subject suffered from powerful withdrawal symptoms. Whatever the test ape 12-19 was suffering from, the strongest vaccine they had—even with its flaws---wasn't working. This wasn't good. Vincent knew they were trifling with forces they had no business fucking with. The day he was told to study the top secret red liquid he'd acquired from the high ranking military general, Bradley Fuller, he knew he was in for trouble. That was nearly six months ago and the government never divulged where they got the base solution, what it was, or anything concrete about its origins, for that matter. It worried Vincent at first. Their lab was supposed to study holistic medicines—natural herbs and remedies. After one look at the compound they'd been given, he knew that they were breaking new ground. He just hoped it was for the better.

Vincent walked over to the cage where test subject 12-19 lay on his side. The ape's chest rose slowly as he struggled to breathe. Vincent frowned as he looked at the discoloration around the ape's eyes, nose, and mouth. The black skin had turned an ashen gray and looked to be dry and crusty.

"You said you gave it six milliliters of VH-32?" Vincent asked.

Dr. Philip turned around. "Yes, and that was twenty minutes ago. It's still not working?"

"No. I think the subject is dying. If anything we've learned from this is that compound RTX-52 counteracts whatever definitive properties are in the VH-32 and VH-12. If it's showing this sort of adverse results in the ape, it will most likely have the same effects on human DNA," Vincent pointed out.

Philip walked over to the cage to check in on their test subject. The animal was clearly in pain, but it was far too weak to move. Every few seconds it released a pitiful whimper or moan. They studied the dying ape with frowns on their faces. It was customary to give the animals numbers. To give them names would create personal bonds and, as scientists, they couldn't afford to have sympathy for the animals in their care. Human lives depended on their objectivity and skill to remain on task. Still, seeing the animal lying in the cage suffering put both men in a shameful state knowing they were the cause of it. They had never lost an animal test subject before. Their usual experiments never produced these kinds of deadly results. This whole situation was taking its toll on everyone and everything involved.

"Maybe we should put it out of its misery?" Philip suggested.

"I wouldn't do that, doctors," Dr. Henrick intervened, coming up behind the two men. He peeked into the cage and groaned. "Even though test specimen 12-19 may be dying, we still need to study the length of time it takes for the ape to die. As a matter of fact, we should inject another specimen... perhaps 04-16 to see how long it takes them to die without the aid of VH-32 and VH-12."

"I'm not going to subject another animal to the whims of our own errors or curiosity," Vincent protested.

"We're scientists, Dr. Masterson. Acting on our curiosity is in our blood," Dr. Henrick countered.

"That may be, but I'm going to disagree with that plan. We need to figure out how to save the one that's already dying before we condemn another to death simply to satisfy *your* morbid *curiosity*," Vincent snapped.

Dr. Henrick practically snarled at the insult. "It's not my 'morbid curiosity' as you've incorrectly stated that is behind my motivation. We don't know what compound VH-0 is. All we know is that it's powerful and unlike anything else on the face of this earth. Where did it come from? Was it extracted from a plant of some sort? Did it come from a human? We need to study the RTX solution if for nothing more than a weapon we can have against the VH-0."

Vincent didn't say anything for a while as he thought about what Dr. Henrick proposed. It wasn't a bad idea. Truth was, what they didn't know about the VH-0 compound could set them back further. Vincent often speculated about the origin of the compound, as did the other scientists. Where did it come from? That was the big question. What if it did come from a human with a rare blood disease—a rare blood disease that seemed to be the cure to every single ailment known to man and could also drive you crazy or kill you or both. Would it be such a bad thing to have a counter to this unknown substance? He looked at his fellow scientist, Dr. Pierce, for his opinion.

Philip shrugged a shoulder. "He's got a point. But more importantly, since this stuff is so addictive maybe we can work with the RTX-52 compound to dilute the addictive properties in the base VH-0 solution?"

Dr. Henrick pointed at Dr. Pierce. "Exactly. For all we know this may be some new drug that's already out on the streets. Or if it's not out already, it may very well be soon. It's going to need a detox chemical to counter its effects."

"One that doesn't kill the patient," Dr. Philip added. "Or drive it insane."

"Look, what you two suggest makes sense. But for now, let's focus on what the funding is actually paying for. The government wants us to come up with a solution that can give its solders superhuman abilities. They're looking for something that will increase the healing process, as well as their speed, strength, stamina, and heighten their senses and cognitive reasoning. So far, all we have is a highly addictive drug that can heal diseases and injuries, but it leaves the subject highly irrational and out of control," Vincent said, wanting to get everyone back on task.

"At least we've made some breakthroughs. The subjects aren't dying anymore," Dr. Henrick stated flatly.

"That, and the VH-0 solution and all its derivatives have proven to be too strong," Vincent said.

"We need to figure out just what the hell we are missing." Dr. Henrick scratched his head with the tip of his ink pen as he pondered.

"Very well. Let's get back to work then," Dr. Philip said, walking back to his desk.

Vincent looked at Dr. Henrick. "Anything else?"

"Of course not, you're the lead scientist on this project. I follow *your* orders," Dr. Henrick replied with more derision in his tone than necessary.

Vincent's brow creased. "You have a problem working for me, Dr. Henrick, I'm sure other arrangements can be made. SciTech does have positions available on Level One."

Dr. Henrick jerked with the mention of a possible demotion. Level One was for the scientist whose main focus was maintaining proper plant growth. The study of different grades of soil was their thing, it wasn't his.

He cleared his throat. "No problem at all, Dr. Masterson."

With that he walked away back to his desk, keeping his

mumbled curses below earshot level. Vincent eyed the man a moment longer. He could practically feel the venom the man no doubt spewed forth in his honor. He could hate him all he wanted, but it was his lab, his rules. The last thing he wanted to do was have conflict with a co-worker with so much at stake. He checked in on the ape inside the cage still struggling to breathe. Its heart rate was slow and erratic. There was no change from a few minutes ago when he examined the animal. Being more optimistic than rational thought would suggest, he was hoping the animal was stabilizing. However, he knew in his best judgment, the animal was simply dying a slower more painful death. He'd check in with the animal in another hour to see where its vitals were at. Until then, it was back to the drawing board.

Chapter Two

"Oh no, you don't. You're not going to come to my party with that same gloomy frown you had on your face all day at work yesterday," Richard said as he handed his buddy a cold beer.

Vincent shook himself. "Man, I'm sorry. Shit at work has been on my mind, ya know?"

"Leave that shit at work, then. Come on, it's a beautiful day. The grill's hot and flaming up some great-tasting ribs—you know I put my special sauce on those bad boys, too. So there's nothing to be frowning about, get the lead out of your ass."

He nudged him and then pointed to two beautiful women standing near the punch table. Sarah was five-six with shoulder-length blond hair and baby-blue eyes that seemed to brighten the room whenever she walked in. Her skin was not only the color of the sweetest cream, but it was just as smooth to the touch. Linda, the other lovely lady, was five-nine with legs for days. Her beautiful chocolate complexion shone brightly under the heated rays of the sun. Both women turned looking at their mates and giggled.

"Ah, looks like their sharp, predatory senses picked up male eye-contact. Look, they're coming in for the kill," Richard joked. "Darling!" He embraced his beautiful wife, Linda.

"Mm hmm, now I know you were over here up to no good," Linda said, kissing her husband lovingly.

"Naw, babe. I'm just trying to get this one here to relax and have some fun," Richard nudged Vincent's arm.

"I'm relaxed enough. I can't help it if I have things on my mind. You're not on a ticking time bomb schedule like I am. You can afford to party hard. I can't. I've got to be at the lab tomorrow morning," Vincent reminded his friend.

Richard took a swig of his beer and saluted Vincent with the bottle. "Fair enough."

"Still, let's have some fun now before you have to leave me tomorrow morning," Sarah said, giving Vincent a tender kiss on the cheek.

Vincent smiled at his fiancée. "All right, I can't disappoint you." He clinked his bottle of beer with his friend's and took a swig.

Richard walked away to check on the meat searing on the grill. He flipped the slabs of ribs over and basted them with his renowned homemade barbeque sauce. Other friends who came to the party mingled with each other, some standing over the grill with Richard either admiring his culinary skills or the grill itself. Others wanted to point out the spots he missed on their desired pieces of meat.

"I'm going to have to ask you to shut the hell up, Ryan. You're cramping my style," Richard joked.

"What style? You know I love the small ends a little burnt, make it happen," Ryan retorted.

Richard pointed the barbeque fork at him. "Keep it up and you'll get the bones from everyone else's plate."

Everyone watching the two men engaging in their ribbing laughed at the idle threat. The music was blaring—various hits of the times along with a few oldies but goodies. Michael Jackson's "Thriller" in particular had the party goers imitating the historic dance sequence. They laughed, ate, drank, and danced for hours and hours until they felt it was a decent time to leave without having to be thrown out by their hosts.

With an unsteady gait, Vincent walked over to Richard, giving him a hug and pat on the back.

"Thanks for having me over, man. It was nice and just what the doctor ordered."

"I knew you'd have a good time. Linda and I are going to throw a little something-something later on this month. You're invited to that, too, ya know," Richard said.

"If I'm not working that day, I'd love to come."

"What do you mean, 'if you're not working'? It's a barbeque at my house, man. My famous sauce alone is reason enough to play hooky on any normal workday. Besides, it'll be on the weekend, kill the overtime and make it happen. It won't be a party if my BFF ain't here," Richard said as he and Vincent walked toward their two women.

Vincent made a drunken off-handed gesture. "Okay, okay, I'll be here with my appetite."

Richard laughed as he balanced Vincent in front Sarah. "It's good you didn't get loaded like this guy here," he joked as he handed Vincent off to his fiancée.

Vincent wrapped his arm around Sarah's shoulder. He leaned over kissing her on her temple. "You ready to go, baby?"

"With you in this condition, you're going to be sorry in the morning," Sarah laughed and then looked at her watch. "Wow, it's that late already. Time really flies when you're having fun. It's almost one in the morning."

"I know," Vincent said with a chuckle.

"All right, all right." Sarah smiled. She wasn't quite ready to go as she was having a great time chatting it up with Linda as always. But Vincent had to be at the office by seven and he was going to need to sleep some of the night festivities off as much as possible.

"I'll see you later, sweetie," Linda said, giving her a kiss on the cheek. "You too, hun. Take care of my girl." She gave Vincent a friendly peck on the cheek as well.

"Don't worry, I will." Vincent took his fiancée's hand and led her out of the backyard toward their Mercedes Benz GLK.

"That was a lot of fun," Sarah said as she climbed inside behind the wheel.

"Yeah, it was," Vincent agreed as he slipped on his seat belt.

Sarah kicked on the ignition and shifted the car into gear. She looked over at her fiancé, his eyes studied the road, focused but weary. She patted his leg, gaining his attention.

"Are you okay?" she asked.

Vincent smiled. "Yeah, I'm fine, baby. Just tired, that's all..." He paused and with a lopsided grin added. "And maybe a little bit drunk."

"Well, you are that." She giggled then grew serious. "Are you under a lot of stress at work? Is that asshole, Morris riding you again?"

"You guessed it. But it's nothing you need to concern yourself with. We're coming very close to making a breakthrough and all will be well soon enough," Vincent said reassuringly.

Sarah caressed the side of his face, gently rubbing her fingers down the length of his jawline. "I love you."

Vincent smiled. "I love you, too."

She drove to their condo on Roosevelt Road near Downtown Chicago. It didn't take long to park and get up to their two-bedroom condo. Both were exhausted after the long workweek prior to the exhilarating party. Vincent was first to brush his teeth and don his pajamas. After that, he practically fell into the bed. Somehow he managed to get under the covers. Sarah followed suit and she slid closer to Vincent, wrapping her arm around his waist and laying her head on his chest. He smiled and pulled her closer as he drifted off to sleep.

***

Aaron tossed off his Regency Hotel uniform on the back of his loveseat. He walked the rest of the way to his bathroom naked. Leaning over, he turned on the shower, adjusting the knobs to get the perfect temperature. He liked it hot, hotter than most people could stand it. Climbing inside the shower stall, he pressed his forehead and hands on the tiled wall in front of him. The hot water cascading down his back felt extraordinary and he released a soft moan in satisfaction. He stood under the steaming spray for what seemed like forever before he actually started to bathe. Once he was done with that, he climbed out and toweled off. Naked still, he walked to his closet and fished through the many outfits that hung on the rod looking for one he thought would make a statement.

The charcoal gray suit with a black silk shirt and silver tie caught his attention. It had cost him more than half his paycheck, but when he saw it on the mannequin, he just had to have it. He'd seen a lot of the other guys wearing similar suits. He didn't doubt theirs were way more expensive, but he had to start somewhere. He dressed quickly, snatched up his wallet and keys and left the apartment.

It didn't take him long to get to the best nightclub in the city— well, the best in his opinion. What was a pain in the ass was finding a damned parking spot. All the ones on the street were taken and that left the parking garage. The expensive, never give you a damn break, parking garage. He pulled up to the entrance in his Hyundai Elantra and read the fee chart.

"Are you fucking kidding me," he cursed as he noted the after-hours price. "Twenty fucking dollars? I ain't staying here long." After two hours, the price when up ten more dollars. He pushed the button, got his ticket and drove forward once the bar rose. It didn't take long to find a spot. He parked and climbed out of his car, adjusting his suit accordingly. The line outside the club was long and he was hoping his friend was minding the door this evening. He was. Luck was on his side this night.

"Hey Aaron, didn't think you'd come around tonight," Jesse greeted along with a masculine handshake that involved a slight chest bump.

"Yeah, I almost passed on tonight. I'm pulling an early shift at work tomorrow, trying to make a little extra on the paycheck, you know what I mean?" Aaron said, chuckling.

"Hell yeah, ain't nothing wrong with that."

"So, are they here tonight?"

"Oh, you mean the Elite?"

Aaron blushed a little and shrugged a shoulder.

Jesse shook his head. "Man, you've got a real hard-on for them."

"Who doesn't? Don't pretend it's just me. Everyone who walks through these doors wants to be where they are," Aaron pointed out.

"Yeah, but not everyone can be where they are. I'm comfortable where I'm at. Sometimes having power ain't a good thing."

"Bullshit."

"Hey, I'm just speaking for myself."

"Bullshit. You're trying to tell me if they wanted you in their inner circle, you'd tell them, 'thanks, but no thanks'?" Aaron cocked an eyebrow as he waited for his friend's response. One he was prepared not to believe.

"I'm saying sometimes it good to be insignificant to some people. Once you're on their radar, you never know what they'll ask of you."

"Spoken like a true chump."

"I guess your ass wants to wait in the back of the line tonight, right?" Jesse taunted. "I plan on letting little, gray-haired old ladies in the club before I let you in, jerk."

Aaron laughed. "Don't be that way. So are they here?"

"Oh right, that's how this little conversation got started." Jesse sighed. "Yes, bootlicker, some of them are here."

"Fuck you for calling me a bootlicker."

"Fuck you for calling me a chump, just 'cause I'm not about to readily kiss ass if I don't have to."

"Fair enough." Aaron conceded. "So, can I go in, buddy?"

"Yeah, yeah, have fun." Jesse removed the red velvet rope and let his friend inside the club.

Aaron walked into the main interior of the club. Red velvet and black satin—as clichéd as you want to be—the club was still very stylish in spite of its pretentiousness. There was a certain level of elegance in the décor. Crystal chandeliers hung from the high ceilings along with crystal balls that reflected multicolored lights throughout the club. Red velvet booths were lined with the club's patrons. Some were chatting. Others were in various levels of making out—one or two to the point of needing their own room. It was the norm for a club like this. Decadence, passion and debauchery. It was *The Den* and he loved it. That's why he'd been trying to get a job there for over a year and, even with his friend putting a good word in for him, he was still unsuccessful. He knew he had to prove himself worthy to the owner.

He looked around the club towards the VIP section, and there they were. Well, some of them, like Jesse had said. He recognized the one people called Chloe right away. She was easy to spot since she had her male plaything, Patrick, faithfully by her side. His collar fastened securely around his neck and the leash held lightly in her delicate fingers. No one dare try to take him from her and the boy-toy wouldn't dare leave her side. To her right were the Twins.

The fucking Twins. If he believed the rumors about them, they had more blood on their hands than Capone's mafia. By their side was Veronica and, if the rumors were true about her, she was as bloodthirsty and freaky as her twin lovers. Aaron couldn't help but be fascinated by their relationship. How did both men enjoy sharing the same woman? And how did she like being with two men who looked exactly alike? He shook the thought from his mind. He didn't want to be caught staring.

He looked around some more and sighed. That was it. Three of the Elite inner circle, but the not head honcho himself. Cassian wasn't around tonight. He was the one Aaron had dressed in his best for.

"Shit," he mumbled.

"Hey, handsome," a female slipped her arm around his waist, gaining his attention.

He turned around, facing her. She was pretty, brunette, blue eyes, with a delicious body. Totally fuckable and just what he needed after the day he'd had.

"Hey there, sexy," Aaron said, offering her his charming smile.

"So are you here by yourself?" she asked.

"Yeah."

"Good. My name's Allison."

"Aaron. Listen, do you want to get out of here?"

"I thought you'd never ask." She gave him a come-hither smile as she led the way to the exit. He followed her and gave his friend Jesse a wink as he passed. It didn't take him long to get to his car and back to his apartment for a little more fun before the sun rose and his shift started.

Chapter Three

Vincent's cell phone started ringing, jarring both he and Sarah out of their slumber. He unwound himself from her and staggered out of the bed, searching for his tan Dockers with his phone in them. He found the pants discarded carelessly in the chair by the vanity. He snatched them up and fumbled through the fabric until he located the pocket with the ringing phone.

"Hello?" he barked in an irritated tone.

"You know you're late to work right? But I'm glad I caught you, I think I made that breakthrough we were hoping for," was Philip's eager reply.

"Philip?" he asked, still discombobulated.

"Yes, it's me and I need you down here right away."

"All right, all right I'm on my way."

"See you soon."

The two men ended the call and Vincent checked the clock on his cell. It was 8:28 in the morning. Philip was right, he was late for work. Had Philip not called him when he did, there was no telling how long he would have slept. His head throbbed courtesy of the hangover from his extensive partying just hours before. He knew he should have called it quits after his third beer. This day was going to be hell, but he hoped it was worth it.

"Is everything all right?" Sarah asked with her face still buried in the pillow.

"Yeah, might be some good news after all, sweetheart. Shit, I'm late as hell and my head feels like a jackhammer's gone out of control," Vincent said as he walked toward the bathroom.

Sarah was far too exhausted to pry any further. Her eyelids fluttered closed and she was fast asleep before Vincent got into the shower. He climbed out and dressed quickly; then scooped up his keys, wallet and ID badge before leaving. It took him a little longer than usual to make it to SciTech labs with the morning rush hour. Because his average work day started at 7:00 AM, he normally beat the traffic. He parked in his designated spot, checked in with security then made his way to the sixth floor where his lab was located. After donning his decontamination suit and going through the process, he entered the highly restricted area.

"Okay, what was so important that you had to drag me out of my bed at 8:00 AM?" Vincent was cheerful in spite of his headache.

"Good morning to you, too, sunshine," Philip replied. "And what do you mean, 'drag you out of your bed'? You should have been here over two hours ago."

Vincent gave him a crooked smile. "Yeah, I know, but you see I was stuck behind this guy driving a Mustang slower than my grandma walks—and she uses a cane."

Philip chuckled. "Is that so?"

Vincent nodded. "Yeah, I hate when I see a slow driver behind the wheel of a fast car. Imagine how the car feels being shackled to someone who doesn't fully appreciate its value. It hurts my heart." He placed a hand over his chest for emphasis.

"Uh huh, is that the only reason you were this late, Mr. Philanthropist?"

"Well, I may have partied a little harder than I thought last night." Vincent held up two fingers an inch apart to indicate the amount.

Philip nodded. "Ah, yes... that'll do it." He chuckled. "Listen, the sweet talk was nice, but now it's time to get down to business."

"That's why I'm here. What's up?" Vincent asked, approaching him.

"I went back to the drawing board and took a look at the RTX-52 compound. I added three ounces of the RTS-14 to a five-ounce mixture of the RTX-52. And then I added two milliliters of VH-0 to the solution. But the real gem came when I added four milliliters of an AB positive blood sample from an anonymous donor and that seemed to neutralize those troublesome G-cells we saw in the VH-0 and its derivatives." Philip gave Vincent a toothy grin. He was quite proud of himself for having made the breakthrough they'd all been searching for.

"How did you figure it out?" Vincent asked relieved that he finally had something he could present to the board and the military next week.

"Well, I can't take all of the credit, I wish I could, but Dr. Henrick's theory about the VH-0 played a huge part in the discovery," Philips said, standing there with his chest stuck out and full of pride.

"Wow, this is wonderful news. I can't believe you figured it— wait a minute—what do you mean an anonymous donor? What are you talking about?" Vincent asked. What Philip said about the blood sample finally registered.

Philip held up his hands, pleadingly. "It was a theory I'd been working on silently. I didn't want to bring it to you or Dr. Henrick until it panned out. Like I said, I'd been thinking about the VH-0 and how its properties resemble human blood, but it's also like a blood borne pathogen. As far as the human donor is concerned, I didn't necessarily go through the proper channels to get the sample."

Vincent's arched an eyebrow. "You stole it?"

"Not exactly. I have a friend that works at the local free clinic. People go in there all the time and donate blood. I just asked her for a small sample from someone who may be under the influence of drugs. Well, to be more exact, I asked her for several samples of blood that seemed to be healthy, but with some form of narcotic present. She was able to narrow it down to a few donors. At home, I ran my tests until finally one was successful and neutralized the compound. I don't know why that particular blood sample worked when so many others didn't. That's the next thing we need to figure out," Philip said. "I'm sure you can understand why I didn't want to tell you about this right away. If things went wrong, you could have plausible deniability."

"Really? You want me to honestly believe you were protecting me in this scheme?"

Philip lips pursed. "Regardless of what you believe, had this been a failure, or I was discovered, you would have been telling the truth by saying you had no knowledge."

"I'm sure you just wanted the credit," Dr. Martin Henrick chimed in.

"This breakthrough means success for us all. What with Morris breathing down our necks, threatening to take the lab from us if we lose this contract. I did what needed to be done." Philip pointed at his chest. "*I* took the risk for the team and I think a *thank you* is in order."

Vincent sighed. "We're going to have to explain how we figured out the missing element and it can't be the blood of some nameless donor. If this is successful, the military is going to want a lot more where that came from and we need to be able to produce it."

Philip nodded. "That's why I suggested we need to find out more about that blood sample."

Vincent nodded. He didn't have a good feeling about what Philip had done, but he did have to admit the other man was right. They were running out of time and he really didn't want to lose control of the lab. That promotion was one he worked hard for; he earned it, damn it! The department head director, Dr. Steve Morris, had been holding it over his head the entire time they worked on the project. In his own words, he had told Vincent, *"I gave you the lab; I can take it away if I don't think you're ready for it."* Needless to say, the pressure was on, but breaking the law was something he didn't want to resort to. *Maybe that's why Philip did it,* he thought. Still, how deep was this hole they were digging? And where in the hell was it going?

"Are you still with us?" asked Dr. Pierce.

Vincent blinked, coming out of his deep thought. He nodded.

"Have you tested the new solution on our subjects, yet?" he asked, getting back on track. He'd have to deal with their other problem later.

"Not yet," Dr. Martin Henrick said, looking up from his

microscope and swiveling around on his stool to face the two men. "We were waiting for you."

"All right. Let's get the video feed ready and, Dr. Henrick, could you prepare test subject 08-15?" Vincent directed.

Both men went about completing their directives. Philip loaded the camera to record the results of their test. Martin pulled a female monkey infant from her cage, gently placing her on the sterile stainless steel table.

"All right, let's start off with one milliliter of the… what are you calling it now?" Vincent asked Philip.

"PVM-1. Simple, I know, but it's in honor of the three of us," Philip said.

Vincent chuckled. "Well, I suppose then I can't knock you for your lack of originality. PVM, eh? Our first name initials?"

Philip nodded.

"I had suggested Elixir-21, but he shot that down," Martin said.

Vincent laughed. "Why Elixir-21?"

"If this thing does what we want it to do—what we're being paid to make it do—then it's no doubt the ultimate elixir made in the twenty-first century," Martin explained.

"And you called me unoriginal," Philip teased.

"All right, gentlemen, let's see if we're going to make history or not," Vincent said. "Let's start off with one milliliter of PVM-1."

Philip filled the syringe with the dark red liquid that looked almost black in the plastic tube. Very carefully, he injected the needle into the chimpanzee's vein and pushed the serum through. The chimpanzee was silent at first, looking very curiously up at the three men standing over her. Philip removed the needle, tossing it into the bio-hazard trashcan.

"Put her back into the cage, we'll observe her from there," Vincent said.

Martin did as he was told, and put the chimpanzee back into her stainless steel cage, locking the door securely. They monitored the ape's vitals from wired sensors they had connected to the sticky pads on her chest, arms, head and legs.

"Does everything look normal?" Vincent asked Philip who was

watching the monitors and checking for any increase in the beeps and multicolored lines that ran across the screens.

"So far, there hasn't been a decrease in vitals, and that's a step in the right direction," Philip said.

"Let's try something else," Martin said.

He walked over to a contraption used to test the animal's strength. He opened the door and tied one end of the device to the chimpanzee's arm. Then he closed the cage door, locking it again. He turned the machine on and immediately, the ape reacted to the low pulse electrical current, pulling back on the strap of the machine as the machine pulled back in a game of tug-o-war.

"Well, there's something. The test subject's strength has increased by about thirty-seven percent from her last readings," Martin said.

"Her adrenaline levels have increased by five percent," Philip added.

"That's good. This is definitely progress," Vincent said with a satisfied smile.

They watched the ape pull on the cord even harder.

"Okay, that's impressive!" Philip commented.

"What happened?" Vincent turned from the ape to take a look at the monitors.

"From these readings, she has the strength of an adult male chimpanzee," Philip said.

"That is impressive. This is what the military wants, what the government wants. Soldiers with this kind of strength—I honestly don't know if this is a good thing, or bad," Vincent commented.

"She's removing the band," Dr. Henrick said.

Philip and Vincent turned back to the ape in the cage just in time to see her unfasten the rubber strap around her arm.

"Unbelievable," Vincent said in a hushed voice.

"They've never been able to figure out the mechanic of that band before and she just takes it off just like that. My God..." Philip said as he ran a hand through his hair.

"Okay, so far we've seen an increase in cognitive reasoning and strength. How about her healing capabilities?" Martin pointed out.

"The test subject seems to be of sound mind, I don't see any irrational behavior... still, I don't think we should remove her from the cage," Vincent said.

"Oh, I wasn't going to even think about doing that. Not without a sedative, at least," Martin said.

"I don't want to give her a sedative until we test her healing capabilities. We need to see if she can heal instantly without the interference of another drug designed to slow down her functions," Vincent said. "I'll make the incision."

Vincent approached the surgical drawer and removed a sterile scalpel. He turned and made his way over to the cage where the female chimpanzee watched him innocently with big brown eyes. She made excited noises as he came closer then wrapped her fingers around the bars of the cage. Very gently, Vincent stroked her exposed fingers as he spoke to her in a soft, calming tone. He raised the scalpel and made a small incision on her index finger. The ape yelped and pulled her hand away from the cage. All three scientists leaned forward, observing the wound as it healed instantly.

"Gentlemen, I think we've just hit rock star status in the medical world," Vincent said, beaming with joy. "Do you know what this means?" he asked, looking from one man to the other.

"It means the United States will definitely have the advantage and other countries will no doubt try to replicate the elixir," Philip said.

"It means we are going to be famous. This thing we created will put us on a whole new level. There's going to be billions involved with the demanding production of this product. We'll be able to name our price," Vincent said. His smile widened as he thought about the possibilities.

"Not only will the military benefit from this, but with a more diluted version of it, we can heal every disease known to man without the extra benefits of turning a human into a super soldier," Philip said.

"Well, we aren't there yet. That's our next step. The good news is we've achieved our primary goal." Vincent patted Philip on the back. "We wouldn't have come this far without your brilliant mind. Now we need to figure out how to cover our tracks and make our research valid and above all, legal."

"We need to study the subject to make sure this success isn't temporary. Or if it is, just *how* temporary," Philip said.

"No doubt, but let's enjoy phase one; bask in success," Vincent joked.

Philip smiled. "Why not."

"I have an idea..." Martin began.

"What is it?" Vincent inquired.

"Philip mentioned using this elixir to heal the sick. Why don't we test it on Subject 12-19? He's still alive, but barely. Why don't we inject the new serum into him, see what effects it may have?" Martin asked.

"I think that's a good idea. We'll see if it can heal someone gravely ill," Philip said.

"More importantly, I want to see the effects PVM-1 has on a subject that has already been infected with other variations of the compound," Vincent said.

"Curiouser and curiouser," remarked Henrick as he nodded toward Vincent.

"It's more than my curiosity, Doctor. If we can save this ape, I think we should try," Vincent said, having caught the sly comment.

"That's wise, too," Philip agreed.

"I agree. If it can cure him where the other serums couldn't, that would be an even greater success," Martin suggested.

Vincent didn't see the harm in it. "Let's do that."

The three doctors walked over to 12-19's cage; looking inside. The chimpanzee was in the worst shape it could possibly be in. There were bald spots on the ape's arms, legs, stomach and back where the fur had fallen out. Puss-filled abscesses had opened on the ape's face and chest oozing a greenish-yellow foul smelling fluid. The ape was lethargic as he lay helpless in the cage, unable to open its eyes. His chest barely rose as he struggled to breathe, wheezing with every breath.

"Oh my God," gasped Vincent as he looked at the sickened primate.

"That's the same reaction I had when I came in this morning," Philip said.

"Give him two milliliters of the PVM-1. If it works, it'll save his life… hopefully. If not, we inject him with twelve milliliters of sodium phenobarbital," Vincent ordered. If they couldn't save him, he'd at least put the beast out of his misery once and for all.

"All right," Philip said. He filled another syringe with the serum and made his way back to the ape's cage.

Martin opened the door and exposed the ape's arm so he could give the injection. Philip slid the needle into the ape's vein and emptied the syringe. The ape released a tiny whimper and then fell silent. Even its chest ceased its unsteady movement. The long beeping sound on the monitor meant only one thing. Subject 12-19 had passed away.

"I guess we were too late," Vincent said with some measure of regret.

"Call the time," Philip said.

Martin looked at the lab clock. "9:45 AM."

"Make sure to write the notes on specimen 12-19 and the effects of compound RTS-14, RTX-52 and the immediate reaction to PVM-1," Vincent said.

"Sure thing." Martian nodded. He looked at the ape again. "He really did look bad, didn't he? Truth be told, I'm actually happy he's out of his misery."

"Aren't we all," Philip commented.

"Indeed. All right, disconnect the wires; get a few biological samples from him. I want blood, skin, fur and flesh," Vincent ordered. "I'll make the arrangement to get the body out of here."

Martin reached over to disconnect the wire attached to the ape's right pectoral. The ape's eyes shot open revealing black irises. It took hold of Martin's wrist, gripping it with the strength of an ape twice its size. Martin screamed as the fragile bones in his wrist began to snap and break under the extreme pressure. The ape sat up quickly, and bit deeply into Martin's forearm. Martin screamed louder as he struggled savagely to wrestle away from the animal. The animal's teeth were embedded deeply into his flesh. Blood bubbled up from the wounds around the ape's canines. Then the ape reared its head back, ripping away flesh and muscle. Blood splattered Martin's upper body coating him. Philip ran as fast as he could over to Martin, grabbing hold of his elbow and doing his best to pry Martin's arm from the ape before he could attack again. Vincent joined them as Martin fought the dizziness that threatened to black him out.

Martin remained conscious as he assisted Philip and Vincent in prying his wrist away from the ape's grasp. He screamed again as pieces of his skin ripped from his body as he pulled away from the animal's grip. Once the doctor was free, Vincent slammed the cage door closed as fast as he could, locking it in place.

Philip aided Martin who was holding his bleeding arm, trying to apply pressure to the wound.

"Jesus Christ! I thought the damn thing was dead. We need to get you to the hospital. Hurry, come on," Philip suggested, ushering Martin toward the exit. "We have to decontaminate you, Martin!"

"Oh God, look at it," Martin said as he looked at the wound in his arm. The skin around the bite began to turn a sickening yellowish color.

"What the hell?" Vincent said as he saw the instant discoloration on the doctor's wound. "We need to get him to a hospital right away." He ran over to the telephone, dialing 9-1-1.

The ape in the cage began to screech and rattle the bars as it tried desperately to break free.

"Holy shit! Look at him!" Philip said as he darted glances from the festering wound to the ape in the cage.

"We need to get him out of here, now!" Vincent yelled to Philip as he kept his eyes on the ape. He began to back up towards the others as they made their way to the exit.

Martin held the tattered remains of his bio-suit to his wound as he made his way through the decontamination chamber with Philip's assistance.

"The ambulance is on its way, we need to get you downstairs to wait for them. Security is on their way," Vincent informed them after catching up to the two men. He stood under the decontamination spray with the others.

"God, there's so much blood, I think he's bleeding out!" Philip gasped, looking at the wound.

"God, I feel sick… we need to tell the hospital about the two compounds when I get there," Martin said. His legs grew weak and he nearly fell, but both Philip and Vincent caught him, hoisting him up and supporting him by the waist.

"That's top secret, I don't know if you can divulge that kind of information. Just tell them you were bitten by a lab animal and if they need it, do what you have to do, but you didn't hear that from me," Vincent advised.

Martin nodded and looked up as soon as SciTech security rushed toward him.

"Please get him into the ambulance that's on its way," Vincent instructed.

"Yes sir," one of the security guards said, taking Dr. Martin by his arm. They walked away and Vincent and Philip went back through the decontamination chamber, then back into the lab. Vincent watched the ape as it struggled wildly inside the thick steel cage. He'd never seen an animal in such a mindless rage. A part of him was mesmerized, but he knew that what he was seeing wasn't normal.

"You need to see this," Philip called out urgently to Vincent.

"What is it?" Vincent asked, rounding the table to look at the monitors. He studied the screen for several seconds and then he saw it. "Oh my God."

"I know, it has no heartbeat and very minimal brain activity," Philip said.

"The hypothalamus and primary motor cortex show highly active signs of activity… but no other parts of the brain seem to be active. Not to mention the lack of a freakin' heartbeat. Are we really reading this right?" Vincent asked as he frantically looked over the several monitors then back at the ape that was yanking as hard as it could against the bars of the cage.

"There's a little bit of activity in the cerebellum, but not much, not enough to explain why a dead animal is moving," Philip said. His heart pounded like a jackhammer in his chest as he attempted to wrap his mind around what had just happened and what he was currently seeing.

"What in the hell is happening here?" Vincent asked the question to no one in particular. He looked at the ape, the very animal that by every law of science known to man was legally dead. How was it possible that it was screeching and raging inside its cage? Its creepy black eyes focused hard on both doctors as it foamed at the mouth.

"We need to sedate it and find out why it's still alive when it shouldn't be," Vincent said.

"I think we need to do that right now, it looks like it's about to break out of that cage," Philip added.

Vincent nodded as he rushed over to the cabinet that held their medication and sedatives. He pulled out an injection needle, loading it into the gun chamber. The animal inside the cage smashed its powerful forearms against the bars, finally breaking through.

"Oh shit!" Vincent yelped as he moved to the far end of the room, still struggling to load the gun.

The raging chimpanzee leaped on top of the stainless steel table then over to where the monitors and Dr. Philip stood with the desk the only barrier between him and the ape. The ape leaped again, crashing its full body weight against Philip. Both fell back over the chair and Philip fought desperately with the animal, flipping the desk over in the process and sending the computers and monitor screens crashing to the floor.

Vincent ran around the surgery table, aiming the gun at the ape just as it bit into Philip's chest and ripped away flesh. He shot the ape with a double dose of etorphine, hoping to render the animal unconscious if not permanently dead. Philip held his hands out, trying desperately to keep the animal at bay. The ape lunged forward again, unaffected by the sedative and bit deeply into

Philip's neck. Rearing back its head, it tore away flesh and cartilage as it severed Philip's jugular. Arterial blood spurted from the open wound, splattering the ape, Philip, the wall and the floor.

Terrified, Vincent ran into the decontamination chamber just as the animal set its sights on him. He stood horrified by what he'd just witnessed. Never had an animal had the strength to break through the reinforced steel bars of the containment cages. He stood with his back pressed firmly against the other exit door as the chemical mist washed over him. As he stood there, the ape began to slam against the first door rattling it on his hinges.

Vincent screamed as he pulled on the handle of the second door, struggling to get out before the ape broke through. The ape pounded repeatedly on the door, rattling the handle and the glass in the window. Vincent's stomach was constricted into a ball of tangled knots as he waited for the chemical rinse to complete its process so the automatic lock on the door would free him. Finally it was done and the lock released. Vincent turned the handle and bolted free, slamming the door behind him. He ran over to the medicine cabinet, pushing the heavy furniture with all his might in front of the door. Once it was in place, he took several steps back, struggling to catch his breath. He knew he had to warn security, so he turned around, locating the emergency button on the telephone.

"Yes, Dr. Masterson?" the security person asked upon answering the call.

"We've got an emergency, sixth floor in my lab! We need to call the police! Dr. Pierce has been killed by one of our test subjects. You need to bring heavy artillery; the animal is very strong and fast," Vincent said in a rush of words he hoped were clear enough that they understood his urgency.

Clearly, they did because the security guard announced that he was on his way up before ending the call. Vincent didn't want to be anywhere near the monster ape. He still didn't understand how the animal became resurrected. It didn't help matters that the animal was stronger than any normal chimpanzee its age and size. He ran into the hallway to look through the thick glass window into the lab. There he could see the ape tearing into what remained of his friend, Philip. His stomach lurched and he had to swallow hard to keep down the donut he ate for breakfast.

Security rushed up the stairs and met up with him in the hallway.

"What's the situation?" the head security chief asked, as he took the safety off his 9 mm.

"Ah, the ape… it killed him. I… I…" Vincent stammered as he tried to find the right words to prepare the men for what they were getting themselves into. "It's dangerous and you have to kill it. Be careful, it's very strong and fast."

The security guards looked through the window and saw firsthand the carnage that Vincent had tried to describe. They couldn't believe it. Never in the history of SciTech Labs had anything like this ever happened.

"Jesus Christ," one of the officers gasped.

The ape looked up from its meal, face and fur matted with bloody bits of flesh. Muscle and shredded skin clung to the ape's open mouth, dripping more blood and bits onto its chest and floor. In a fit of blind hunger the animal raced toward the glass throwing itself at the pane. The men standing there watching the animal jumped backward, shocked by the animal's aggression. The ape lunged again and the glass shuddered under the powerful force of the animal's weight.

"Holy shit! It's trying to burst through!" One of the officers belted out.

The ape lunged again and the glass cracked in a spider web pattern, splitting from the middle and branching out in crooked lines to the edges.

Several employees stepped into the hallway, curious as to the ruckus taking place.

"Please get back into your labs, for your own safety," ordered the head security chief as he monitored the ape's attack.

Some of the people watched the scene for a bit before doing as directed. A few went so far as to lock their doors. The more curious lot continued to watch the situation unfold.

"It's not going to hold up," Vincent yelled as he stumbled several steps back.

"Get ready, boys," the security chief said, preparing his men to take the animal out. They stood their ground as the animal threw itself at the glass several more times, finally bursting through. The sound of gun shots vibrated throughout the hallway as they fired at the animal. Bullets struck the ape, ripping gaping holes in his chest cavity, but the animal didn't fall. It leaped forward, smashing into the head security officer and biting into his cheek, ripping the skin away. The man screamed as blood gushed from the wound. Other officers fired at the animal, filling its torso with as much lead as their guns could hold. The ape pounced from the security chief's chest onto another officer, bringing him down to the floor. The man slammed the butt of his handgun into the ape's cranium but the animal didn't fall off. Again the animal bit into the officer, greedily chewing and tearing the flesh of his neck and shoulder.

The man released a gurgled scream as blood bubbled in his open mouth spilling down the side of his jaw. The employees who had been watching were now fleeing toward the elevators and emergency stairwells. Some went back into their own labs for protection. Two other officers ran back several paces as they frantically reloaded their guns. After loading a new clip each, they aimed and fired again and again at the ape, drawing the animal's attention. It ran towards them, leaping into the air and landing on one of the guards. The man screamed as the ape bit into his shoulder, taking a huge chunk of flesh and muscle. The officer fell against the wall and slid to the floor as the animal began devouring him as he lay there, helpless.

Vincent watched in horror as the last security guard ran away, down the hall. He couldn't believe what he was seeing. The guards had put enough bullets into the ape to kill a wild elephant, yet the ape seemed unaffected.

The sound of glass falling on the floor drew his attention towards the now shattered observatory window.

"Oh my God!" he gasped when he saw Philip's half mutilated

corpse climbing through the broken glass window. One of his legs had been ripped off and the white bone was exposed surrounded by bloody tissue and cartilage. Then the once deceased security chief sat up and both sets of their lifeless, cold, black eyes stared directly at Vincent.

The chief sprung to his feet and ran toward Vincent with a wild look in his piercing gaze. Vincent had all but a half a second to gather himself enough to run like hell down the hallway towards the emergency stairwell. He flung the door open and raced down the stairs leaping four to five steps at a time. He didn't bother to turn around to see if the dead security chief was still behind him, he didn't need to. He could hear him coming closer.

"Run!!!" Vincent screamed as he pushed past co-workers in the stairwell who appeared to be unaware of the danger. Vincent didn't stop to see if anyone took heed to his warning. He could hear the screams of the terrified individuals as he made his decent. Once Vincent reached the bottom level, he slammed through the door, knocking down his director, Steve. The coffee the man had been carrying went one way and the man went the other.

"What the hell?" Steve looked at his breakfast as it fell out of the bag. "Vincent what's going on?" he asked.

"Run!" Vincent yelled at the man over his shoulder. He didn't stop running until he got to his car. Frantically, he searched for his keys only to realize he'd left them and his wallet in his jacket which was still in his locker. He turned toward his boss who was making his way over to him.

"Where's your car?"

"What the hell is going on?" Steve asked again.

Just then another employee came bursting through the back stairwell covered in blood as it poured from her open neck and arm wounds. With the same glazed, wild look in her eyes, she focused on the two men and ran toward them.

"Fuck! Run!" Vincent yelled as he took his own advice.

His feet hit the pavement as fast as a piston putting as much distance between him and SciTech as he could. He needed a car.

He needed to get to his fiancée. He needed to figure out just what the hell was going on. Several blocks away, he caught himself on a traffic light. He snatched the helmet of his bio-suit off, dropping it as he doubled over and struggled to catch his breath. His heart raced so fast, he doubted if it would ever slow down. His head throbbed and the nausea he'd been fighting for the past several minutes finally won out. His stomach lurched and everything he'd had that morning and the night before reintroduced itself before spilling out on the pavement before him. Someone walked over to him, seeing him covered in his protective gear.

"Hey, are you okay, buddy?" the stranger asked from a safe distance away. "Do you want me to call an ambulance?"

Vincent spit the last of the bile onto the puddle before him and wiped his mouth with the back of his hand. He looked up at the man and nodded. "I need you to call the police, tell them there's been a chemical outbreak at SciTech Labs and they have to contain the facility immediately."

"Oh shit!" the stranger said, pulling out his cell phone and fumbling to flip it open. He also made sure to put even more distance between himself and the sick man wearing the SciTech Lab bio-suit. He placed the call, telling the police everything the man told him to say. "I swear this isn't a fucking hoax!" he added.

"We know sir, we've already received several calls from SciTech Labs and we're working now to resolve the situation. Thank you for your call," the dispatch officer said. She made sure to get the man's location and information before ending the call.

"What did they say?" Vincent asked the man.

"She said the police already know about it and they're taking care of it."

Vincent shook his head. He had no idea what "it" was but he was putting what faith he had left into the Chicago police department.

"May I borrow your cell?" Vincent asked hand extended.

"Ah, look buddy, I don't want to get involved," the stranger said as he began retreating.

Vincent watched as the man ran to get away from him. He

couldn't blame him, but he really needed a telephone right now. Shit! Where was a pay phone when you needed one? In this age of wireless devices, pay phones were all but extinct. He took a few glances behind him to see if any dead people were on the streets. So far, so good. Maybe the police were their best bet. Still, the Center for Disease Control needed to be notified just to be on the safe side. He ran down the street a few more blocks, still putting distance between himself and SciTech. People—curious and suspicious of him still fully dressed in his white, blood-splattered lab bio-suit—avoided making contact with him as he passed by. He could feel their eyes on him, but he made certain to keep moving forward. There was a part of him that wanted to yell "run for your lives" but that would either grant him even more arch-eyebrow expressions or start a mad panic, so he opted to remain silent as he searched for nearest telephone.

***

"So, how about doing a little sight-seeing after the convention?" Dr. Felicia Anderson asked her two colleges Dr. William Bale, a tall, handsome African-American male, with short cropped hair and hazel eyes, and Dr. Samantha Grey, a cute blonde with shoulder length hair and blue eyes, as they waited in line at Starbucks.

"Hell, if we have any damn time left before we have to head back. This damn convention's going on for six more hours. I hate these fucking things sometimes," William commented as he took another step forward getting closer to the counter.

"I don't know, I kind of like them. I haven't gone to many, but I always find them informative and it's nice to meet up with a few familiar faces in the field," Samantha said, giving her colleagues a different perspective.

"Nerd," Felicia teased with a coy smile.

"Don't hate," Samantha retorted. "Damn, how long does it take to pour coffee at a coffee shop? This line is taking forever. I was hoping I could get a Cappuccino before we have to get back."

"I think they have to wait for the guy to come back from Columbia with the beans," William joked.

"He must be traveling by mule," Samantha added.

"Shit, girl, I don't know." Felicia chuckled at her two co-workers. "They need to open up another line. They know this is still the AM, people need their caffeine fix." Felicia stepped out of the line slightly. Making sure the people behind the counter would be able to see her; she raised her voice, "Is there a manager back there that can assist with opening up another line?" She tried her best not to sound as pissed off as she felt.

"You're bad," Samantha whispered with a mischievous flare.

"I'm tired of waiting in this damn line," Felicia clarified.

Apparently, the management took the hint and opened up another line, to which several people, including the three of them jumped into right away.

"Squeaky wheel gets the oil." Felicia smiled. Just then, her cell began ringing, blaring the rhythmic melody of Jasmine Sullivan's "I Bust the Windows out Your Car". It let her know that her boss was calling. With a slight grown and roll of her eye, she rubbed her thumb over the screen, answering the call.

"Hi, Dr. Washington," she greeted.

Her co-workers shared knowing looks. Each of them knew Dr. Bryant Washington was the last person on earth Felicia wanted to talk to today. He was the main person responsible for sidelining her promotion. As far as Felicia was concerned, it was because he wanted to keep her working under his supervision. It was suspected that the good doctor had a bit of a crush on his sexy female counterpart. In any case, he was on her shit list.

"We may have a bit of an emergency. I can't tell you how serious it is at the moment, because the reports I've been getting aren't consistent, but apparently there's been an outbreak at SciTech Labs and we've been getting calls of a similar outbreak at Mercy Hospital. How close are you to either of those locations?" Dr. Washington asked, getting right to the point.

Felicia took a look out the window, noting the street signs. "Well, I'm closer to Mercy Hospital right now. We'll head there and try to get things under control. What kind of outbreak is it? What are we walking into?"

"Honestly, I don't know. Be prepared for a violent environment from what I'm hearing. I've got reports coming even as I speak with you about people eating people, if you can believe it."

"Come again?" Felicia asked with one eyebrow cocked.

"Hey, I hear you. I'm not sure how much of this I'm willing to believe myself. But then again, I'm not there. So I need you to go to that hospital and report back to me what you find."

"We on our way," Felicia said as she rose from her chair, followed by her two companions.

"Be careful," Dr. Washington cautioned.

"Don't worry, we will." She ended her call, slipping her cell back into her pocket.

"So what's up?" Dr. William Bale inquired.

"I'm not one-hundred percent sure," Felicia said. "We have an assignment to check out Mercy Hospital. Apparently there's been an outbreak. From what he told me, might be some kind of drug that makes people go insane and eat each other. I have no idea. I'm going to contact the police and make sure we can have a few units there to meet up with us. If this situation is as violent as I'm made to believe, we're going to need some firepower."

"So much for trying to get in a little sight-seeing after the convention," William commented. "Or the convention, for that matter."

"Look around, because that's as close as we're going to get," Felicia replied as she waved her hand at the approaching cab.

They climbed in and gave the driver the hospital's address. Felicia called the police department and told them who she was, her credentials, and where she was heading.

"We already have police officers at that location, ma'am," the dispatcher informed her.

"Who's the officer in charge?" Felicia asked.

"That would be Sgt. Peter Kominsky, ma'am"

"Thank you." Felicia ended the call.

"So this *is* really serious," Samantha said.

"Dwayne seemed nervous enough." Felicia looked down at her cell phone as it started ringing again. She answered. "Hello?"

"Dr. Felicia Anderson?"

"This is she, whom am I speaking with?"

"I'm glad I caught you. My name is Dr. Michael Bloomberg from the Illinois Department of Public Health. We received a call from Dr. Dwayne Washington at CDC, who gave me your number. He informed that that you're on your way to Mercy Hospital. I'd like us to meet up before you go in there. A lot of the calls we've received are very strange."

"One minute." Felicia looked at the cab driver. "Excuse me. How far are we from Mercy Hospital?"

"With all this traffic, about ten minutes, maybe less," the cab driver answered.

"Thank you." Felicia put the cell back to her ear. "We're about ten minutes out. We'll meet up with you once we get there. I was told a Sgt. Peter Kominsky of the CPD was in charge at the scene."

"He was, no one has heard from him since he went into the hospital. At least that's the latest report I have."

"What do you have so far?"

"Apparently, there's a very hostile virus that is causing rabid and psychotic behavior in those infected. I've got reports of people biting and killing each other with their bare hands. From these reports, it would seem that in their uncontrolled state, the infected are stronger physically and highly irrational, almost like a dog infected with rabies, or a person on PCP."

"Those are similar to the reports the CDC received," Felicia said.

As they got closer to their destination, they began to hear the sound of rapid gunfire and see the signs of sheer panic. The driver stopped his cab, unable to go any further do to the traffic jam. People were abandoning their cars and running in the opposite direction.

"What the hell?" Felicia murmured as she looked out the window at the panicked people running by.

"Um, I think this is as far as I'm taking you. Are you sure that's where you want to go?" the driver asked. His voice wavered, showing signs of the fear and uncertainty he was feeling.

"We have to. This will be fine," Felicia said as she paid him the amount on his mileage meter. The three scientists climbed out of the cab and immediately started making their way toward the hospital. They passed more people running in the opposite direction—some of them in hospital gowns and nothing else.

"What the fuck?" William watched a man in a wheelchair roll himself away as fast as he could. He was still in his hospital gown with his oxygen mask on his face and an oxygen tank on his lap.

"Dr. Bloomberg, how far are you?" Felicia asked as she tried to remain unperturbed by all of the chaos surrounding her.

"I'm pulling up right now. I can't get close to the hospital because of all these cars. I'm about three blocks away."

"We're about five blocks and we're on foot," Felicia said. "Do you have any protective gear?"

"Yes, we have a mobile unit with us."

"Excellent, we'll need to borrow some of you resources."

"Of course."

"We'll see you soon." Felicia ended her call, slipping her cell back into her blazer pocket.

"I don't like the way this shit looks at all," William said as he kept up his fast pace.

"You and me both," Felicia agreed. "I think that's them."

The trio ran towards the team of people who were suiting up in white bio-suits complete with helmets.

"Is there a Dr. Bloomberg here?" Felicia asked as she approached them.

"I'm Dr. Bloomberg. Dr. Anderson, I presume."

"Yes." Felicia flashed him her badge. Her colleagues did the same.

"Good." Dr. Bloomberg said after giving each badge a quick inspection. "The suits are in the truck. I think we have just enough for the three of you."

"Perfect." Felicia said.

"Maybe one of you should stay behind. Here," Dr. Bloomberg handed William his truck keys. "Just in case."

"Are you sure?" William took the keys apprehensively. He cast a glance at Felicia then back to Dr. Bloomberg.

"Keep an eye out. It's just a precaution." Dr. Bloomberg turned toward Felicia and Samantha. "All right, my team and I are going in now. We have walkie-talkies and once we're in, we can give you an update."

"All right." Felicia nodded as she stepped into the bio-suit.

"You should wait to hear back from me before you go in," Dr. Bloomberg advised.

"We're coming in there soon, you just stay safe---Jesus!" Felicia gasped as the sound of gunfire echoed throughout the area.

"Yeah, we've been hearing a lot of that." Dr. Bloomberg looked toward the hospital entrance as more police officers rushed in. "Please, wait until you hear back from me," he pleaded.

Felicia looked at him. She saw how sincere he was and nodded. "All right. We'll wait until we hear back from you. But if I don't hear back from you soon, I'm going in."

"Fair enough." Dr. Bloomberg turned and walked toward the hospital with his team.

Felicia and her team zipped up their bio-suits as they watched his team enter the hospital. "Be safe." she gave them a silent prayer.

***

Vincent was relived to finally get a stroke of luck. After making numerous attempts at several different businesses lining the street whose front desk employees took one look at his attire and then promptly asked him to leave, he eventually found a hotel where the receptionist allowed him to use the telephone. He contacted the CDC and when he got a hold of someone, after he confirmed who he was, he told them about SciTech Labs. They patched him through to one of the administrative personnel who was more than eager to speak with someone from SciTech Labs.

"My name is Dr. Bryant Washington, Assistant Surgeon General and Director, Office of Public Health Preparedness and Response, and your name?"

"I'm Doctor Vincent Masterson, a head-researcher at SciTech Labs. My director was Dr. Steve Morris. Look, I know you have no reason to believe I am who I say I am, but I swear I'm not lying. We have an emergency outbreak in Chicago and we need to contain it as soon as possible," Vincent said in a rush of words he hoped were coherent enough.

"We were just made aware of the situation, Doctor Masterson. We've received several telephone calls from other employees of SciTech Labs, hospitals, as well as our contacts from the Illinois Department of Public Health." Dr. Bryant Washington informed. "We received a call from a Dr. Richard Benton, who informed us about your possible involvement. He mentioned that you and your team were working on a secret military project and that your lab received a distress call this morning, one of your doctors was injured?"

Vincent gave a silent prayer; thanking God that Richard was still alive. At least he hoped he was still alive. He had to bring himself back to the present to focus on the doctor's questions.

"That's true. I am directly involved with what's going on," Vincent replied. "One of my doctors was seriously injured and was rushed to Mercy Hospital. The other was killed by one of our infected test subjects."

"Mercy Hospital is the second location we've been receiving calls from. I've just sent a team there and we're sending more units as fast as we can to St. Noel Hospital as well as SciTech Labs and several other locations where outbreaks have been reported."

"What?" Vincent gasped as he struggled to comprehend how quickly the epidemic was spreading. If an epidemic was what it was—he didn't even know how to define it.

"What can you tell us about the situation since you're directly involved?" Dr. Washington asked.

Vincent had to gather his thoughts before he could answer him.

He was still reeling from the fact that several locations were already under attack in so little time. He shook his head to clear his mind when he heard Dr. Washington repeat his name. "I'm sorry. How many places have the outbreak now?"

"SciTech, Mercy General Hospital, St. Noel Hospital, a McDonalds, and several other locations," Dr. Washington informed.

"Dr. Washington, I can't understand what is actually happening with this outbreak. For me to fully explain everything or even how we can come up with some sort of vaccine, I need to get back into SciTech Labs. Unfortunately, at this point, it's impossible. I barely escaped with my life. I need to get to a safe location and people need to evacuate the city as fast as possible."

There was a slight pause as Dr. Washington reflected on the new threat. "Where are you at now?"

"I'm standing in the lobby of the Regency Hotel, but I can't stay here. I need to get back to my condo and gather whatever research I have on my hard drives and then my fiancée and I have to get the hell out of the city," Vincent said. His voice rose an octave as he struggled to keep calm.

"We don't need you creating a panic among the residents of the city—"

"There's already a panic, Doctor. It's been less than an hour and already several places have been attacked and more of those things are rising up and killing," Vincent pointed out.

"Let me connect you with our team of doctors who are already in Chicago. Perhaps you can meet up with them," Dr. Washington suggested, not really certain what the right move should be.

This wasn't like any other outbreak he'd ever heard of. It wasn't like anything he'd ever experienced. He wasn't sure if normal protocols were going to help. Already, he had received a telephone call from Dr. Michael Bloomberg, one of the head researchers at the IDPH regarding the state of affairs in Chicago and from what he had described, it seemed like the End of Days was just beginning. He put Vincent on hold while he connected the call to Felicia's cell phone. He made the introductions quickly before demanding an update.

"I'm preparing to go into Mercy Hospital with my team," Dr. Felicia Anderson said, bringing her boss up to date. "Dr. Masterson," she began, addressing the other man, "the more you can tell us about this highly unusual outbreak, the faster we can contain it."

"Dr. Anderson, as I've told Dr. Washington, I really don't know what it is. I can't explain it. All of my research is located on the sixth floor of SciTech Labs, room 608. Even with all of my research, I can't explain how the dead are walking."

"Did you just say the dead are walking?" Felicia asked, hoping she misheard him.

"That's exactly what's happening. We need to evacuate the city as soon as possible. The people infected with this—whatever it is —are extremely strong and fast." Vincent did his best to give them the information he'd gathered just by his own observations.

"We haven't heard any reports of dead people walking again, Dr. Masterson--"

"--Listen to me, it's obvious the reports you've been getting are seriously lacking in information. I've seen with my own eyes, people who've been killed get back up and start attacking anyone in sight," Vincent said.

"Fine, I won't argue. Can you tell us anything? Like what happened? How did this start?" Felicia asked.

"One of our test subjects died as a direct result of a failed experiment. Before it died, we tried several vaccines—new vaccines to restore its health—but none of them worked. Shortly after the test subject 12-19 died, it came back to life. No heartbeat, no pulse and very little brain activity. The only parts of the brain that seemed to be working were the primary motor cortex and the hypothalamus," Vincent said, remembering the brain activity he saw on the monitor before the ape escaped.

"That would explain why—" Felicia was cut off by someone screaming in the background. "What's going on? Talk to me, what's going on?!" She was yelling at someone through a two-way receiver.

All three of them could hear the static over the screams through the telephone line.

"Get out of there, pull back. Get back to the truck," Felicia said, giving her best instructions.

There were more screams and crying over the static, then the unmistakable sound of the walkie-talkie hitting the floor. Felicia knew that the doctor from the IDPH who'd been trying to give her updates had dropped the radio. Over the telephone both men could hear the shrill, panicked screams from what sounded like hundreds of people in the background. They waited impatiently for Felicia to return to their conversation and update them.

"Dr. Anderson, what's going on?" Dr. Washington asked, his tone concerned and urgent.

"I... I don't know. A team of doctors from IDPH went into the hospital to help control the situation, but I've lost contact with them. One minute." Felicia tried to contact the doctor again. "Dr. Bloomberg, are you there? Are you all right?"

There was no response. Both Vincent and Dr. Washington listened very carefully, hoping to gain some understanding about her current predicament.

"Listen, if you can hear me, just get the hell out of there," Felicia urged.

Vincent listened to the background chaos. There was no mistaking the sounds of people screaming in fear and confusion and running for their lives. Whatever was happening was going to be heading his way and soon. He needed to get back to his condo. He needed to get to his fiancée. More importantly, he needed to get the hell out of Chicago.

Several painfully terror-driven moments passed before the two men on the telephone heard Felicia scream Dr. Bloomberg's name.

"Felicia, I think you need to worry about yourself and your team, get the hell out of that area, it doesn't sound safe," Dr. Washington stated.

"One minute, someone's coming out..." she paused. "Oh my God! Let's get out of here!"

Vincent jumped when he heard the urgency in her terror-stricken voice. He could only imagine what she was seeing. If it was anything like what he'd witnessed at SciTech, then he knew that the situation was not under control—far from it actually.

Both men on opposite sides of the phone could hear the unmistakable sounds of gunshots blasting away and people running, and they suspected she was on foot.

"Get in and drive! Drive!" Felicia yelled at her companions as they fled.

The two men could hear the automobile's door closing and the engine start. Next they heard the screeching of tires.

"Felicia! Felicia, are you alright?!" Dr. Washington yelled through the phone which caused Vincent to have to remove the headset from his ear.

"Yes. Sam and William are with me, we made it out of there. Thank God Dr. Bloomberg suggested William stay behind or else we wouldn't have made it," Felicia said.

"What happened?" Dr. Washington asked.

"You were right, Dr. Masterson. Those things aren't people any more. They're monsters. They came pouring out of the hospital and started attacking the police right away. Dr. Bloomberg was one of them. The way he looked ... all mangled ... oh *God*. I didn't see much after that, we just ran as fast as we could back to Dr. Bloomberg's truck," Felicia was still panting heavily as she spoke. "Doctor Masterson, where are you? I need to meet you."

Vincent could hear tires squealing in the background and that made him even more afraid. Apparently, they were hauling ass.

"Take the sidewalk! I want to get as far away from that place as possible!" Felicia instructed whoever was driving the truck.

Vincent couldn't blame her. "Right now, I'm at the Regency Hotel on Michigan Avenue. I'm in the lobby, but I'm not staying here. I can't risk it. Meet me at my apartment." He gave them the address.

"We're on our way now," Felicia told him before hanging up.

"Dr. Masterson, when my team gets to you, gather everything you can get your hands on that can help us. I'm sending a helicopter within the hour to get you all out of there," Dr. Washington informed.

"Oh don't worry, I will. Thank you." Vincent ended the call, not bothering to tell him that he wasn't going anywhere without Sarah. He looked at the clock on the wall, it wasn't even noon. He hoped that she was still at home instead of taking her usual morning jog. He had to try to contact her. He had to reach her. If she wasn't at home, then she was caught up in whatever the hell was going on out there. He had to know if she was safe.

Vincent turned around when he felt two pairs of eyes burning figurative holes through the back of his skull. He looked at the two hotel receptionists who were now staring back at him with worried expressions having overheard at least *his* side of the conversation. During the intensity of his phone conversation he had forgotten all about them. He was surprised that they were still standing there.

"I'm surprised you're still here, you all need to leave," Vincent said, putting his thoughts into words.

The taller receptionist between the two, whose name tag said "Aaron", looked at his co-worker apprehensively before returning his gaze to Vincent. "Um, I'm not sure what I just heard, but it doesn't sound good. Is there something we should know?

"Yeah, is what you were talking about true?" asked the shorter one, whose name tag said "Reginald".

"Shit, I wish it wasn't. Trust me, this isn't a hoax and soon it's going to be on the news if it's not already," Vincent said. He pointed to the telephone again. "May I make one more phone call?"

"Should I get the hotel manager?" Reginald asked.

Vincent thought about what he should tell them. He didn't want to spread panic, but he didn't want to minimize the ever increasing threat. Getting the hotel customers and employees to safety would save lives. Especially since the hotel was only three miles away from SciTech labs. But what did that say for the other businesses and residences in the outbreak's wake? He couldn't warn everyone and the news... was the news already alerting people? If it was, maybe people were evacuating.

Vincent looked at the man. "Reginald, right?"

"Yes."

"Yes, Reginald, get the manager and is there a television around here?"

Reginald nodded and pointed to a tavern and grill across the hotel lobby. "The television's located over the bar."

"Thank you," Vincent said. He proceeded to make another phone call. He called the condo first and when she didn't answer, he called her cell. After several rings and a silent prayer, his call went to her voicemail, which frustrated him to no end. Today of all days was *not* the time to have missed calls. To his utter disappointment, he was forced to leave a message for her and pray again that she'd check her phone in the next 5 seconds.

"Damn it, Sarah! When you get this message call me, but get home right away. That's where I'm going. We have to leave the city immediately until the outbreak is under control. Something went horribly wrong at the lab today and I can't explain everything now. I just need you to trust me and do as I say. Get home, I'm on my way."

"Fuck!" he cursed, slamming the handset back onto the base. "Where the hell are you, Sarah?"

He struggled to think of any other numbers he could call to contact her. Just then, the manager walked up to him accompanied by Reginald.

"Hello my name is Mr. Wellington, Regency Hotel Manager. I'm told that you have an important matter to speak to me about?"

Vincent nodded. "Listen very carefully. My name is Dr. Vincent Masterson. I'm the lead scientist of the biological research division at SciTech laboratory and there's been an outbreak. I don't know how many guests you have in this hotel, but you have to evacuate immediately. Please try to do this as efficiently as possible without spreading panic, but it is of the utmost importance that you clear out the hotel."

The manager tossed him a skeptical look. "Sir, you must understand my position. I have no idea who you are, I can't evacuate the hotel because you, a complete stranger claiming to be a doctor, orders me too." He eyed Vincent's bio-suit and the splatters of blood covering it again and was pleased that he instructed one of the receptionists to contact the police department. If it was a terrible hoax or if something more horrible had happened, he wanted the law to be involved either way.

"Sir, I think the threat is real," Aaron said. "He's already called the Center for Disease Control." It was his best attempt to convince his boss to take the matter as seriously as he was.

The manager looked at him, eyebrows raised in shock. He turned back to Vincent. "Do you have any credentials? Any paperwork to confirm anything you're saying?" He had no idea how he was going to evacuate an entire hotel on the premise that they needed to leave the city immediately. Again, that was providing this wasn't some elaborate hoax.

"I'm sure it's on the news, turn on a damn TV!" Vincent blurted out without really meaning to.

The manager huffed. "I do not fully understand what you're talking about. What kind of outbreak? And wouldn't it be best to lock down the hotel in order to protect the guests if there is an outbreak? We can even offer room comps for our guests if this is an emergency."

"Look, I have to get out of here. Doctors from the Center for Disease Control are on their way to meet up with me," Vincent said. "I'm not fucking around here. There may not be enough time if you wait; this outbreak is spreading faster than we can contain it. Please, sir, I'm begging you, evacuate." He didn't bother to wait around any longer to see if the hotel manager took his advice. He ran out of the hotel and immediately bumped into a woman dressed in a business suit. He fell back against the hotel door from the impact and she landed on her side, skinning her thigh.

"I'm sorry," Vincent said, bending down to help her up.

She quickly scrambled to her feet with his help. "You need to run!" she warned him and then did just that, leaving her purse on the ground at his feet.

Vincent picked up her purse.

"Wait, you dropped your purse," he yelled, but she never turned around. Taking the purse with him, he continued running down the street towards his Michigan Avenue condominium.

Chapter Four

Aaron watched as Vincent crashed into a woman right outside the hotel. The lady ran off, leaving her purse and Vincent ran off in the same direction. He couldn't help but notice even more people running past the hotel's glass doors and having heard a lot of the conversation Vincent had, he knew something big was going down.

The first thing he wanted to do was warn Cassian, but damn it, he didn't have his phone number! He knew where he lived, they all did but getting there was going to be difficult if what that doctor said was true. And from the look of Vincent bloody clothes, it was.

"Do you believe him?" Mr. Wellington asked Aaron, bringing him out of his contemplation.

"I think we should either evacuate the hotel, or lock it up," Aaron suggested.

"I'm inclined to agree, but there's no way we can evacuate this entire hotel. That just isn't feasible. I need to make some calls before I can make that decision," Mr. Wellington said, then he turned heading back into his office.

Reginald looked at Aaron. "I don't know about you, but I'm started to get pretty fucking freaked out."

"Yeah, you ain't alone," Aaron said as he looked around. "I don't care what he said. We need to lock those fucking doors." He came from behind the desk and walked straight to the doors, locking them up.

"Are you crazy, he's going to be pissed at you," Reginald chastised.

"Right now, I couldn't give a rat's ass. You see that shit out there?" Aaron pointed towards the people running by the doors. "That shit's real. Those people are scared out of their fucking mind and I'm not taking any chances waiting around for that stupid bastard to make the right move." He walked back behind the desk.

"Excuse me, what do you know? What's going on?" One of their hotel guests asked. As if on cue, other guests began to approach the desk. They watched people running by the entrance doors and Aaron could see the panic starting to rise among the crowd.

"Please, people calm down. I have secured the doors and no one is getting inside. There's been a reported outbreak and we're doing whatever is in our power to keep all of our guests safe," Aaron said.

"Yes, the CDC has told us to lock the entrances to keep those infected from getting in. It's not safe right now for you to be on the streets," Reginald lied, but with good cause. The last thing either man wanted to deal with was dozens if not hundreds of people rushing them.

Mr. Wellington entered the lobby. He wasn't surprised by what he was seeing. He knew it was only a matter of time before the hotel's guests would want answers.

"Did you lock the doors?" He asked the two men.

Aaron nodded. "Yes, just like the CDC instructed." He decided to go along with the original lie.

"Good." Mr. Wellington addressed the growing crowd that had gathered in the lobby. "Please people, remain calm. It would be best if you all returned to your rooms and keep your door locked. We have to clear the lobby right away. Please return to your rooms and don't worry, we are waving the room fee until this situation is resolved."

There were murmurs among the guest, some wanted to leave, but were too frightened. If the Center for Disease Control had instructed they stay inside, maybe that's what they should do. Good news was, the rooms were free... food, too, probably.

"What about the food, is that free?" one of the guest decided to ask.

"Yes, of course. Please return to your rooms and remain calm.

You will be well taken care—what the hell?" Mr. Wellington cut off his own sentence when he saw what was outside.

Aaron turned just in time to see a horde of black eyed bloody humans running down the street. Many were dressed in bloody, torn business suits, sundresses and several were still wearing their backpacks.

"What the fuck?" he gasped. He stared at the crowd, unable to take his eyes away from the sight.

Their piercing wild gaze told him they were no longer the people they used to be. Whatever their plans were for that day, none of it mattered. Suddenly, dozens of them stopped chasing the people running down the street. They began to take notice of the people standing in the lobby in clear view. The first one came running, flinging himself against the thick glass window. The window shuddered under the force, cracking in the process. Others quickly followed, throwing their bodies against the doors and windows in a desperate attempt to get inside. The hotel guests began to scream and run towards the elevators and stairs. Some were either too scared or too curious to move, and stood watching. Aaron jumped over the counter and began shoving the nosy guests towards the elevators.

"Get out of here, go!" he pushed them in the direction away from the doors.

His efforts didn't help. The rabid humans broke through the glass and charged forward. The guests who had refused to run were the first to get attacked, followed by those still waiting for the elevators. Aaron watched in horror as the infected humans chased hotel guests through the stairwell. They were faster and stronger than he had expected and they caught him off guard. He sensed one approaching and he managed to snatch up the letter opener from the desk. When the crazed human rushed him, he plunged the opener deep into its chest, piercing its heart. There was very little blood from the wound which would have shocked Aaron had he had enough time to reflect on it. The thing that used to be a human, still wearing his blood-splattered, Armani business suit, didn't flinch or scream; instead it snapped at Aaron's face and neck as they struggled. The scent of the decaying flesh from its victims clinging to its teeth pounded Aaron's senses, repulsing him. He managed to fling the thing from him, but then he was attacked by four more. He couldn't hold them off and when one of them bit him, everything went black... then red.

***

Vincent shoved his way past people running in the opposite direction while others were standing by, probably looking for the reason why others were so afraid. *What was the saying?* He thought. *Oh yeah, 'curiosity killed the cat'.* Unfortunately, the counter being; '*satisfaction brought it back'*, was a little too close to home as far as he was concerned.

In this case, that kind of curiosity *was* going to kill everyone, and most likely bring them back. He could tell by the loud, ominous chorus of screams, the twisted sound of metal colliding as cars smashed into each other and shattered glass that he didn't have much time left to get to safe place—if his high-rise condo could even be called that. He didn't know much, if anything, about these new creatures. He did know that his thick oak door wouldn't be a strong enough reinforcement to keep those damn things out. That much he was sure of.

People ran in every direction, bumping into each other as they fought over cabs and struggled to get onto buses to get away from the downtown area. Vincent dashed across the street, narrowly missing a speeding cab whose driver slammed on the breaks in the nick of time. Vincent didn't waste time bitching, he continued on toward the entrance of his sky-rise condo. He hastily pushed his way through the revolving glass door into the lobby. Instantly, he noticed the security detail was nowhere to be seen. *Pretty smart on their part,* Vincent thought as he walked past the residents who were now evacuating. Soon, he'd be joining them. He hoped. He made his way onto the elevator, pressing the button for his floor.

As soon as the elevator doors opened, several residents shoved past him, forcing their way onto the lift. He had to push his way through the panicked crowd or be stuck having to ride the elevator back down. He managed to jump out just as the doors started to close. Other residences rushed toward the elevator, but not fast enough to catch the ride.

"We have to get out of the city," Henry Baker told him. "It's all on the news, some crazy shit's going on downtown and people are fucking dying!" He paused in his hysteria as his eyes traveled over Vincent's bloody clothes. Slowly he began to back away.

Vincent looked down at his uniform, then back up at his neighbor, who was now   looking at him as if he were an ax murderer. He didn't bother to explain why he was covered in blood. He didn't have the time anyway. Ignoring Henry's questioning gaze and a few other fearful and curious expressions from fleeing residents, he ran down the hallway toward his apartment. He reached into his pocket, his fingers feeling around for the tell-tale metal grooves of his keys and his lucky rabbit's foot keychain... *Shit*.

He'd forgotten again that he left his wallet and keys back in his locker at SciTech Labs. Quickly, he ran back to the elevator, hoping he'd be able to get into the locked box behind the security desk to retrieve the spare key. After several excruciatingly long minutes, one of the elevators' bells dinged and a set of mirrored doors opened. Once again, he was bombarded by residents, this time, they were returning, no doubt for their belongings before evacuating, just like he was planning on doing.

He climbed onto the lift and pressed the lobby button, hoping to get a straight ride down. He didn't. The elevator stopped on several floors, reaching its capacity to the point, two people were shoved off just to get the doors closed. Vincent was pressed painfully against the walls of the elevator. His chest was constricted by the pressure as he struggled to breathe. *Is Fate this resolute to kill me on this day? What the fuck?* He wondered as he considered all of his near-death experiences of the past hour.

Finally, he made it to the lobby and was able to inhale his lungs to their full capacity once the other passengers fled the elevator.

Vincent ran toward the security desk, hopping on the counter and sliding over to the other side with ease. Immediately, he located the locked key cabinet and looking around, found a metal stapler to hammer the little lock with. After several forceful pounds, the tiny latch holding the cabinet broke off and he yanked open the door.

Condo number 4842. It was what he was looking for. Vincent snatched the key off the ring and dashed back over the counter. Just then, three people dressed in white bio-suit complete with helmets circled their way through the revolving door. In the lead carrying a brown purse and a black, metal case was a pretty African-American female with beautiful round eyes that conveyed the amount of concern Vincent felt. She had been talking on her cell phone as she made her way through the lobby.

***

"Wait, are you Dr. Masterson," Felicia asked, eying his blood-splattered lab bio-suit. She knew she was taking a wild guess, but she thought she might have her man.

He walked over to them. "Dr. Anderson, I take it?" Vincent informally greeted.

"Yes, it's him," Felicia replied to the person on her cellular. "I'll call you later." She ended her call, slipping the phone into her purse. "Dr. Masterson, I'm glad we caught up to you. This is Dr. William Bale and Dr. Samantha Grey." She pointed to each person respectively. "We need to leave right now."

Vincent nodded. "That's my plan, Dr. Anderson, but I need to gather my research and my fiancée, she's on her way." At least he prayed that Sarah listened to his damn message and was hauling ass back home.

"We're going to have to make it quick, but the first thing I want to do is decontaminate you as much as possible. Whose blood is that?" Felicia asked as she and the others kept pace with Vincent toward the elevators.

Vincent looked down at his ruined bio-suit. "It belongs to my co-worker, Dr. Henrick. He was bitten."

"So the blood could very well be contaminated?" Felicia asked, stepping back, slightly as did her companions.

"I don't know. Possibly. I haven't had a lot of time to think about it. I've been hauling ass since everything went down," Vincent said.

"I want to take that suit to the lab and have it analyzed," Felicia said.

"Sure, of course." Vincent couldn't help but feel contaminated now that the doctor had pointed it out.

Adjacent from the elevators, the stairway door flew open as a few dozen people rushed through. Some of their luggage was so quickly packed that several articles of clothing hung from the suitcases. The people ran toward the emergency exit door, avoiding the revolving doors as they seemed to take too long.

When the elevator doors opened, several more residents rushed off. They stepped to the side to avoid being knocked over by the stampede. Once the lift was free, they all climbed inside. Samantha's blue eyes bored into Vincent as if she were studying him. As much as he tried to ignore it, she made him feel uncomfortable as if she were judging him.

Vincent nodded at each person. "First off, I haven't had the chance to check the news, but are they getting the word out to the public to evacuate the area?"

"Not at first, because we were trying to contain the situation. But on the way here, I instructed several major media stations to issue an alert for people to stay inside and lock their doors," Felicia said.

Vincent shook his head. "Staying—"

The elevator doors opened on the twentieth floor, Felicia held her hand up, stopping the crowd from getting on. "CDC, this elevator is contaminated, please take another."

The panicked individuals took one look at their white bio-suits, one of them bloody and decided to take her advice. They backed away from the doors and the doors closed.

"You were saying?" Felicia cocked a brow.

"Staying inside might not be enough—" He paused again when

the doors opened.

Like before, Felicia stopped the people from climbing aboard. They made it to the forty-eighth floor and several people rushed them to get on the elevator, hastily rolling their luggage and fumbling with their cell phones as they made calls. This particular crowd ignored Felicia's warning about the contaminated elevator and they pushed past the doctors.

Once again, he found himself fighting the residents to get off. This time he wasn't alone. Felicia and her associates shoved and slid their way passed the herd and managed to jump off the elevators safely.

"As I was saying..." Vincent began as he jogged down the hall towards his apartment with his new companions in tow. "Staying locked inside their homes won't be enough. I've seen these things break through glass windows two inches thick like they were paper. Good news is it looks like the news is finally getting to some people. Leaving is the best option." He slid the key into the lock and opened the door.

Everyone entered and Vincent locked the door.

"That was the last thing I wanted to do—issue an evacuation warning. With everyone trying to leave the city at one time, it's going to create a gridlock," Felicia said. "But I may not have a choice. We don't know what we're dealing with here and the only reason why I'm not hauling you in for an interrogation is because my supervisor tells me you may have a clue about how to fix this."

"A clue might be giving me too much credit. I don't know what the hell is going on. I have some files here that might be able to help me piece some things together," Vincent said, heading into his bedroom with Felicia in tow. He slid out of his bloody clothes revealing a casual wardrobe of dark blue button-up shirt and brown khakis.

"Put those in this plastic bag," Felicia ordered. She had removed a sterile plastic bag from the kit she confiscated from Dr. Bloomberg's truck. She knew it would come in handy.

Vincent did as he was told, putting the bio-suit inside the clear plastic bag Felicia held open. She sealed the bag close and then pulled another two bags out of the black case—one large, one medium size. Then she made a general gesture towards the rest of his clothes.

"You know the drill, Doctor," Felicia said.

"Yeah, I know." Vincent stripped naked, placing his shirt in one bag and his pants, underwear, socks and shoes in the other larger bag.

"All right, I was serious about the shower. If we had the resources, I'd have you scrubbed down really good. We don't know how this virus is being transferred and I'm not letting you take any more chances with public safety," Felicia said.

"It was a matter of life and death. Sorry if I didn't have time to change out of my blood-stained clothes into something more pristine while I was running for my life," Vincent remarked as he walked towards his bathroom.

"It's a necessary precaution, Dr. Masterson," Felicia said in her most professional and no-nonsense tone. "Now, would you prefer Dr. Bale to perform the procedure or me?"

"You," Vincent answered without any hesitation. The idea of having a man scrub down his naked body didn't appeal to him in the least, medical protocol be damned.

"Very well. Step into the shower, please and face the wall."

"Jesus Christ," Vincent fussed. Still, he didn't bother to argue with the tough-as-nails-bitch from the CDC. He stepped into the shower facing the wall and stood under the barely tolerable spray of cold water.

"Ahhh, shit!" he said

Felicia removed a plastic bottle with a cloudy solution inside it. "Do you have a brush?" she said as she looked around the bathroom.

"Sarah's got one of those loofas. That's the best I can do," Vincent remarked.

"This isn't a game Dr. Masterson. I'm trying to save lives and protect people. The last thing I wanted to do when I woke up this morning is scrub a grown ass man down because he may be contaminated with a deadly virus." Felicia reached for the loofa disinfecting it. "Arms up."

He did as he was told. Fighting what he knew was the right move wasn't productive, so he decided to tone down his attitude. Felicia scrubbed down his back, buttocks, thighs and legs. In spite of everything that was going on, a part of him couldn't help but become a bit aroused and this was why he refused to turn around when she told him to.

"Ah, I think I can take it from here... please," Vincent said, peaking over his shoulder. "Like you said, I know the drill."

Felicia caught the hint. She did have to admit, he had a nice ass and package. But that was unimportant to her at the moment. "Fine. But get every crevice." She handed him the loofa and stood back.

Vincent made sure to cleanse his entire body all over again and then he rinsed off. Felicia handed him a towel and he dried himself quickly. He shivered slightly as his body temperature readjusted itself to a normal level.

"We're going to have to work together if we're going to get a handle on this situation, Dr. Masterson," Felicia said.

"I know and I agree completely." Vincent wrapped the towel around his waist, securing it in place.

"Good. I'm willing to hear your suggestions."

"What I really want to do is get to my partner's home before it's too late and retrieve his hard drives and computers..." Vincent paused, his mouth forming a perfect "O" as his eyes bulged from their sockets. "Oh my God! His wife! She has to get out of town, but maybe if I can reach her, she can pack his research data for us."

He ran to his desk, immediately scanning through his digital Rolodex, searching for Dr. Pierce's number. He found it and snatched up the cordless phone, punching the numbered buttons with no small measure of haste. He stood there, listening to the telephone ring several times before their voice mail answered the call, droning out the standard greeting.

"Shit!" Vincent cursed, but still, he left a message indicating how important it was that she gathered her husband's research—as much as she could carry. He ended the call, and then tried his fiancée once again.

This time, she answered.

"Sarah! Oh thank fucking God!" Vincent all but screamed into the telephone.

"Vincent? Oh thank God you're alive!" Sarah replied in a breathless voice.

"Where are you?" Vincent asked.

"I just ran into the building, I'm waiting on an elevator. Whatever the hell those things are, they're coming. I saw them, Vincent. I saw what they were doing. God! Won't the elevator move any fucking faster?!" Sarah fussed as she twitched and fidgeted while waiting for the doors to open. If they didn't open in the next five seconds, she was going to take the stairs. Forty-eight floors, be damned. She's rather die of a heart attack then be eaten alive any day of the week.

"Oh thank goodness! All right, I'm in the condo packing our shit. We're getting out of here," Vincent told her.

The elevator doors finally opened and more people spilled out, pushing past Sarah with absolutely no regard for her toes, shoulders, or anything else on her body.

"Ow! You asshole!" Sarah shouted at one of the men who smashed her big toe under the heel of his sneaker. The man continued on without even so much as a backward glance.

"What happened?" Vincent asked, concerned.

"I'm all right. Considering the urgency of this situation, I'll forgive peoples' rudeness. I should be one to talk anyway, I knocked a few people down and out of my way running to get back home after I got your message," Sarah said. "I'm heading up now."

"Okay, good. I have to finish packing. I'll see you when you get here. I love you so much," Vincent said, feeling every word with all his heart.

"I love you, too." Sarah slipped her cell phone back into her pocket as she watched the level lights turn bright red with each floor she passed. The elevator stopped at several floors and more people climbed on board. They didn't care that it was going up first; they were willing to do that if it meant soon they'd be going back down towards the exit.

***

Vincent went back into his bedroom with Felicia. He pulled a pair of jeans and a black t-shirt from his dresser and dressed quickly. Next he packed a large duffel bag with clothes and items he felt were of the utmost necessity. With one good swipe of his arm, he swept several toiletry items off the shelf in the bathroom into the bag. Toilet paper, toothpaste, soap, deodorant and a box of tampons all went into the bag.

"That will have to do for now," Vincent muttered to himself.

"You want to tell me how all of this started?" Felicia asked her tone straightforward and commanding.

Not really. I swear, how many times am I going to have to go over this? Vincent thought.

Fact of the matter was, he was far too ashamed and no matter how he looked at it, he couldn't shake his feelings of guilt from his involvement.

"I feel like I keep repeating myself. I've already told you everything I know," Vincent said.

"Well tell it to me again. Every. Single. Detail." Felicia stood there, arms crossed over her chest. She waited.

Vincent paused and looked up at her. The entire city was in a fucked up situation because of something he was involved in. He could tell by the look in her eyes, despite her professional demeanor; she was holding him at least partly responsible. Part of him couldn't blame her. Still, he put aside his own issues. They needed his help—whatever help he could offer—not his self-pity. He began to talk as he cleaned out his secret money stash hidden in several books on his nightstand bookshelf.

"The ape was dead, I swear it. There weren't any readings on the monitor. We had just discovered the breakthrough we'd been looking for. It would have revolutionized the world. Heal diseases and strengthen our military force all at the same time. It was going to make history," Vincent said in his defense.

Felicia snorted. "Yeah, well whatever the hell you did *is* making history. So, at what point did it all go wrong?"

Vincent flinched at her bluntness. Destroying humanity isn't one of the things he wanted to go down in history for. Curing cancer—most definitely. Curing AIDS—oh hell yeah! Creating healing rations for soldiers on the battlefield—just hand over the Nobel Peace Prize. But this shit, what the fuck!?

Vincent couldn't really fault her for the harsh dose of truth. He felt he'd earned that and more—maybe a swift kick in the nuts. In all honesty, he couldn't believe his rhetoric himself. He never did have the confidence in their project the other scientists had. Something about it always rubbed him the wrong way and with good reason considering what was going on around them.

"Hey?" Felicia snapped.

Vincent blinked and looked at her.

"Get back to the story please," she reminded.

"I'm sorry," Vincent said, forcing himself to stay on track. "I guess I can always contemplate my hubris later, right?"

"I don't give a damn what you do later as long as we take care of what's happening now," Felicia shot back. "I don't think you're taking this as seriously as you should."

Vincent's brows creased and his lip turned up in a sneer. "Don't presume to tell me what I'm feeling or thinking. You weren't there when I saw my friends get ripped to fucking pieces by that damn ape," he snapped.

"Fair enough. Stay focused then. I need you here," Felicia said, pointing from his eyes to hers with her first two fingers.

Vincent nodded and continued. "Well, the ape bit my colleague..." His voice trailed off as he thought about Dr. Henrick. "My God."

"What?" Felicia asked, turning around to see if he was seeing something she didn't.

"Dr. Henrick, he was the first bitten, the first infected. We rushed him off to Mercy Hospital," Vincent said.

Felicia's expression grew solemn. "That would explain why the hospital was the second call on our radar. It was overrun by the time we got there, as was SciTech. My team and I had met up with a team of doctors from the IDPH. The hospital was surrounded by police and some of the officers had already gone inside. As a precaution, Dr. Bloomberg had suggested William stay behind in his truck to monitor transmission. He and his team went inside; I was on my way to follow them when you contacted me. Had I not received your call, I would have ended up like them."

"What happened?" Vincent asked. He already had an idea, but he wanted to know what she saw so that he could judge just how bad things were.

"They weren't in there five minutes before Michael... Dr. Bloomberg contacted me over the radio. He said something about there's too many of them and that they were fast. I told him to get the hell out of there. I was going to let the police lock it down. We had no idea what to expect going in, I thought it was something we could contain from the inside. Quarantine the infected, you know the drill. We didn't even have time to talk to any of the doctors. No one was left alive inside… well, alive-alive."

"Did the police lock it down?" Vincent asked.

"Those things came out the front door. There must have been over fifty of them. Some of the police officers who went inside were among them as was Dr. Bloomberg." Felicia lowered her head more from guilt, then from grief. "I didn't bother to stick around to see anything more."

Vincent remembered talking to her on the telephone when that all went down, and he understood. She did the only thing she could do. Hell, he'd run as fast as his feet could take him when the bodies started dropping and then rising at SciTech. He didn't even know if Steve got away from the female attacker or not. He never bothered to look back.

"The last thing I saw out the rear view mirror was the rest of the cops being overtaken by those… things," Samantha said.

Both Vincent and Felicia turned when they heard her speak.

"My colleague Dr. Henrick suffered life-threatening wounds

when he was attacked. The arteries in his arm were severed and he was bleeding out fast. Fast... everything happened so damn fast! He must have died soon after he got to the hospital for it to be so quickly overtaken," Vincent speculated. He zipped up one duffel bag and went over to his closet, pulling out another.

"So they rise up within seconds after dying, is that what you're trying to tell me?" Felicia asked.

Vincent nodded as he walked toward the kitchen and into the pantry. "That's exactly what the hell I'm telling you." He looked at his watch. "Where the fuck is Sarah?"

He tossed the bag on the counter and quickly walked towards the front door. Before he could reach for the handle, Sarah opened the door.

"Oh thank God," Vincent breathed as he pulled his fiancée into a tight embrace.

She hugged him back as hard as she could, silently praying that they'd never be parted again. He pulled back and looked over her, checking for injuries.

She noticed what he was doing and took her fiancé's face in her hands. "Look at me, I'm all right. I'm all right," she said, hoping to give him some measure of relief.

"God, I thought something had happened to you. It took you so long," Vincent said, hugging her again.

"That damn elevator must have stopped on every floor on the way up, then it had the nerve to get stuck. It was so frustrating!"

He nodded. "We need to leave as soon as we can. Can you finish packing some food while I gather my computer and drives?"

Sarah nodded.

"Hey, what's your password?" William asked Vincent.

"What?" Vincent turned, seeing the other doctor at his computer desk.

"I need to get into your system to download your files."

"I can take it from here, you wouldn't know what to save," Vincent said.

He walked over to his desk and began packing away Scan Disk

portable drives, his two external hard drives and his laptop. William rose from the chair and Vincent took his place, typing in his password. He stuck another drive into the USB port and began copying files.

"Who are these people?" Sarah called to him from the kitchen as she looked around her condo at the unfamiliar faces.

"Scientists from the CDC, we're trying to get a lid on the situation," Vincent answered.

"The CDC got here that quickly?" Sarah asked, shocked.

"We were in the city for a national health conference, but that isn't important right now," Felicia offered her the brief explanation. She walked toward Vincent standing behind his computer chair. "Are you going back to SciTech?"

Vincent shook his head. "Shit, not by myself. I know we need to get into SciTech Labs to gather what information we can get our hands on. But I don't think we should try to do it ourselves."

"I agree," said Dr. William Bale. "Before we go in there, we need to at least figure out how to neutralize these things."

"Don't you mean, 'kill'?" Sarah pointed out. "It's okay to say that word. We all want to know how to do that."

"Did you see them?" Samantha asked.

"I saw what one of them could do to us. It was horrible," Sarah said, her voice lowering a few octaves as her mind replayed the vision of a mother and her son being ripped apart by one of the... what was the best word to describe them? Zombies?

Vincent had stopped what he was doing on his computer and was studying her. He hated that something he did could make her feel such fear, such despair. At that moment, he was so angry with himself, so disappointed. Seeing how the memory was affecting Sarah, Vincent decided to redirect their attention back to him to take the load off of her.

"From what I witnessed, bullets aren't stopping these things so it's only a matter of time before the entire city is under siege. We need to get to my co-worker's home, Dr. Pierce. He was the one who discovered the perfect compound. We need his research and I'm sure a great deal of it, if not everything, is at his home and the lab."

Felicia nodded. "I'll tell headquarters about Dr. Pierce's research."

"It's not just his research, we have to gather everything. We pumped so many compounds into that particular test subject; I need to be able to separate the variables that mutated its biology. Like I was saying, it was all but dead and then we injected the compound that gave us the positive result we were looking for in hopes that we could cure it of its illness. It didn't work. I still can't understand why not," Vincent said.

"What do you mean... what is this compound?" Dr. Bale asked.

"To be perfectly honest, I don't really know. It was given to us by the military and Gen. Bradley Fuller was extremely tight-lipped about its origins. We were to neutralize its unstable elements to turn it into something we could use to help the human race," Vincent said.

"There's that word again," Sarah mumbled, referencing the word "neutralize".

"Come again?" Felicia asked her, one eye-brow raised.

"It's not important," Sarah begin. "Just a personal gripe I have. I'm not big on politically correct terms that beat around the damn bush and don't mean shit."

"We can debate the legitimacy of politically corrects terms when the city isn't in jeopardy," Samantha said. "Can we please stay on topic," she snapped.

Taking her overstated hint, Vincent continued. "In all of our previous tests, two of the subjects were injected with a tiny sample of the base component so we could see how it reacted with the animal's physiology. Our results were conclusive that the subjects showed an increase in strength, speed, agility and response time. They also healed faster, but unfortunately they became extremely addicted to the compound. So much so, they became unstable and had to be put down."

Felicia frowned. "Unstable how?"

"Highly irritable, for one thing," Vincent answered. "Nothing seemed to satisfy them. There were no treats we could give them that could quench their hunger or their thirst. Even water seemed to give them no relief. They stopped eating and drinking all together and when one died from lack of nutrition and water, we put the other one down to spare him that painful death."

"My God," Sarah gasped.

Vincent looked at her briefly and then looked away, not wanting to see the look of shameful accusation on Sarah's face.

Felicia turned to her. "You didn't know what he was doing for a living?"

Sarah took her eyes off Vincent and turned her gaze to the doctor. "I knew he did research for SciTech Labs. But it was never like this. They worked with natural remedies, things that weren't supposed to kill his test animals. It was supposed to be a cruelty-free laboratory. At least, that's what it boasts about."

"Money changes everything," Vincent began. "I said the same thing, but the contract from the military was... very generous, to say the least. The Board of Directors didn't want to turn it down and neither did our CEO."

"What about you?" Sarah asked as her stare drilled into him.

Vincent lowered his gaze once again. He looked back up at her, eye-to-eye. "I had a moment of weakness. I admit it. I thought with the money my department would get from this experiment, we could do so much more. Then when I listened to what they wanted us to create, I thought it would do the world a favor in the long run even if, in the process of achieving our goals, there would be casualties."

"What about a loss of values and conviction," Sarah shot back.

"I didn't think anything like *this* would happen, Sarah, damn it!" Vincent snatched the jump drive from his computer. "We were trying to help people, save lives. This medicine we created could cure cancer, do you understand me? It could cure AIDS, diabetes and every ailment that has brought mankind to its knees. We had evolved with this discovery, not only for our generation, but for future generations to come."

Sarah scoffed as she shook her head. "And where has playing God got you?"

"Sarah, we had good intentions," Vincent pleaded.

Sarah walked over to him, pressing her hand on his chest over his heart. "I know, baby. I know... you're not a cruel man. It's just I'm so scared and this situation is so horrible. Having good intentions just isn't enough."

Vincent opened his mouth to speak but realized he didn't have the words that could defend his actions, so he closed his mouth and turned towards the other scientists in the room. "I want to fix this situation, but I don't know where to begin or how. The only rational thought I have to offer you is the research. We need to get to the labs. Everything is there, our combined data, and the serums we were working on are also there. I don't know what else to tell you. Whatever we do, we've got to start there. We need those serums and the test subjects that might still be there. They might even be what we need to cure those infected."

"Let's not sugarcoat it, those 'infected' are the dead walking," William said as a matter of fact. "In all honesty, I don't think they can be cured."

Vincent looked at him. "I'm inclined to agree. But the scientist in me would still give it a try."

"What about the human in you?"

"The human in me fearing for his life however, doesn't want to take the fucking chance, if you know what I mean," Vincent replied.

"I know what you mean," William agreed with a knowing nod.

"We need to get to the roof ASAP. We need to get to the Health Department headquarters in Springfield, it's the closest," Felicia said.

"When we get there, we need to find a way to get back into SciTech Labs safely. Hopefully with the time that will pass, the place will be cleared out... hopefully," Vincent said.

"You said you got the base compound from the military right?" William asked.

Vincent nodded. "Yes".

"Did they ever tell you where *they* got it?"

"No, and don't think that I didn't ask," Vincent said. "It was one of the reasons why I started to have doubts about this project. Not knowing the origins of the base compound was frustrating, to say the least. Not to mention, its adverse effects on our subjects were a bit unnerving. Still, we had success in spite of it all."

He wasn't completely willing to forget the fact that they had designed a serum that was revolutionary to the world and were well on their way to breaking barriers in the medical field as well.

"Success at what price?" Sarah asked absently as she flashed back to the sight of the mother and child being eaten alive. She couldn't help but wonder if they were one of those things out there.

"You don't understand," Vincent stated. "We created a serum that could possibly slow the aging process, heal broken bones and every disease known to man in a matter of seconds. Can you fathom what that means?"

"And along the way to your history-making discovery, you created this brand new disease that can somehow resurrect the dead," Sarah accused. "So what we're dealing with is some shit straight out of a horror movie. I dare say zombies."

Vincent frowned, but nodded. "I swear I had no idea anything like this would happen."

"Look, can we play the blame game later. We need to finish getting the research here," William said, ceasing the tit-for-tat that was going on between the two lovebirds.

"I was just doing what I was told to do. I was doing my job," Vincent said in his final defense.

William grunted as he shifted his gaze from Vincent to his companions. He knew full well the ramifications of scientists experimenting with something new and quite possibly lethal in the so-called noble pursuit of doing *one's job*. But this shit was something completely different all together, as far as he was concerned. He seriously doubted the honorable proclamations Vincent spewed forth in an attempt to justify his part in what was going on.

William walked over to the window along with the other two doctors. At the height of the condo, they had a pretty good view of the city and things weren't looking so good. They could see that fires had been set off in several buildings surrounding the location of SciTech labs. Flashing lights of emergency vehicles were scattered throughout the downtown area. Multiple sirens blared in an ominous chorus so loud it was almost deafening even from where they stood.

"What's really unfortunate is the timing of this thing," Sarah said, joining the others in the living room. "Is that it's summer here in Chicago. The Taste has attracted people from all over the country to the city and on top of *all* that, it's a work day. Millions of people in one location getting attacked is not something we need right now, but it's where we're at."

"I'm going to try to call Philip's wife. If she's home, I can get her to pack up his research material," Vincent said, picking up his cordless phone. He dialed the number, but there was no answer. "Shit! I think I've had my fill of people not answering their damn cellphones today."

"Do you think it's spread that far?" Sarah asked "I mean, Philip lives in Skokie."

"It's a possibility, I can't deny that," Vincent said, looking at the other doctors.

"We need to get to the rooftop," Felicia reminded. "Do you have everything you need?" She pointed towards his computer, not really caring about his other provisions.

"Yeah, but it's not all that I need," Vincent reiterated. "We're going to need to bring something with us to barricade the rooftop door once we get there. If those things manage to get in here, they're going to be climbing each level looking for us."

"You mean, for food?" William clarified.

"If you want to put it that way, I guess," Vincent said, with a scowl.

He was on his way towards the hall closet when his phone began to ring. He answered it immediately. "Clare, thank God, you're alive. Is everything all right with you?"

"No. I've been trying to reach Philip all morning, after what I saw on the news, and I can't. Is he with you? Is he okay?" Clare,

Philip's wife asked. Vincent's throat tightened with sorrow as he thought about what he was going to have to tell her. That her husband was the second casualty. That her two children, Thomas and Jasmine would never see their father again, or her, her husband.

"Answer me, damn it!" Clare shouted over the receiver.

"I'm so sorry, Clare, Philip—"

"No. No, no, no, no, please, God, no!" Clare began to scream and cry as one of her greatest fears came to life. She had prayed and held hope that her husband was still alive, but just having difficulty getting out of the city and that's why she couldn't reach him. She hadn't wanted to entertain the thought that he was dead or, worse yet, one of those things running around killing people.

"Clare, I know you're grieving right now. I can't imagine what you're feeling, but you have to get out of there, it's not safe," Vincent urged.

"I have the security shutters down. We're safe, my children and I..." she managed to say through her tears and pain-filled gasps.

"You're not safe enough, Clare," Vincent pressed.

"But those things are already out there, I can't risk it!"

"Jesus Christ, they're there already?" Vincent gasped. The speed in which these things had attacked and traveled continued to amaze and horrify him. "Listen to me. You can't stay there. I have a helicopter coming for me and I want to swing by and pick you up with the kids, but first I need for you to gather up every bit of research Philip had on our secret project. Papers, disk drives, vials of blood, everything."

"What?" Clare asked. Her voice quaked with the fear she felt along with her sadness as she tried to stay focused on what he was telling her.

"Just pack every single hard drive, jump drive, scrap of paper, and modems you can find. Put it in a box. We need his research data, Clare. I can't stress how important it is right now that I see his data. Also, if you find any vials of blood, please pack those too, we need them."

"All right, I'll gather what I can find. Please hurry," she said, the anxiety in her voice seemed to increase from what Vincent could tell.

"I will. Trust me, I'm coming for you and the kids," Vincent promised and then he ended the call.

"What's the ETA on that helicopter?" he asked Felicia.

"I was told thirty minutes, maybe a little less, which is why I said we need to get to the roof."

He looked down at his watch, noting the time. "Good. We need some tools and materials to barricade the door. I don't want to be attacked if we're waiting to be saved." Opening his closet, he pulled out a tool box.

"Getting back on track," Samantha said to Vincent who turned to face her. "This Dr. Henrick was bitten? Is that how you think the virus is being transferred? Through saliva?"

"It would seem so, which is why I think those helmets you all are still wearing are unnecessary."

"Maybe, but I'm not taking any chances this isn't airborne, too," Felicia stated.

"If it is, you've already been exposed."

"Maybe, maybe not." Felicia was standing her ground.

Vincent nodded. "Fair enough. From my own observations, people who were killed by the ape rose within a minute's time with the same glazed look in their black eyes and raging hunger. I don't even understand why they're eating people. Shit, I don't even understand how their cognitive functions are identifying people as a food source."

"That's what's blowing my mind, too," William agreed.

"Their eyes turn black?" Samantha asked.

Vincent nodded. "It happened with the ape and with all the others I've seen. Needless to say, it's a tell-tale sign."

"That's interesting... and creepy," Felicia said, with a slight shiver. "Did Gen. Fuller give you the name for it or did he just call it 'base compound', too?"

"He called it VH-0. We gave it the nickname 'base compound' because that's what it was. We made variations of it during our experiments," Vincent said, checking his watch once more.

"What does VH-0 stand for?" Felicia asked.

"I don't know,' Vincent said. "Gen. Fuller wouldn't answer any questions we presented him. Kept saying shit was classified."

"Well, the military and everyone involved are going to have to open that black box right now. I'm not going for that 'it's classified' bullshit," Felicia commented.

"Hopefully you'll have more pull than we did," Vincent said.

In a moment of pure curiosity, he turned on the hi-definition television to see if the news had any more details on the situation in the city. A reporter stood in front of the camera from what looked to be a rooftop. Behind him looked like a war zone. The Chicago police and the National Guard were firing into a crowd of what Sarah adequately had called "zombies" as the horde rushed toward them. The zombies climbed over overturned and parked cars as they mindlessly made their way toward the firing squad.

"As you can see from the footage, the bullets are not stopping these things. We are trapped on the roof of Dave's Famous Hotdogs on Canal and Roosevelt. Oh my God!" the reporter leaned over the building, observing the mayhem below. "If you can get a look at this, you'll see these things used to be regular people. I mean, my God, there are children among them!"

Dutifully, the cameraman followed his gaze, positioning the camera to capture the activity. It was true. The zombie crowd consisted of children, adults, senior citizens and all were mutilated in some grotesque fashion. Body parts missing, flesh half-eaten, entrails exposed and hanging free. The scene was horrific.

Several infected people were tearing apart the officers and soldiers as the remaining few fired their weapons while in retreat. Two soldiers jumped into their Hummer and backed out down the street at top speed. Their walking-dead attackers kept pace with the vehicle at remarkable speeds, jumping and climbing over the scattered automobiles in pursuit. The cameraman zoomed in as close as his camera lens was capable. The soldier driving the SUV was doing one hell of a job as he maneuvered the behemoth vehicle around scattered and overturned automobiles. Eventually, they were able to put distance between themselves and the zombies and the horde split up, running down the cross-intersection street at top speed.

"You saw it here. These things are incredibly fast and strong," the reporter said. It was in his voice and his eyes, he was terrified. They all were. "Jesus Christ, look at this." He motioned for the cameraman to follow him and he did.

One officer and two soldiers who had been fatally attacked began to rise. First sitting up and then springing to their feet as if choreographed. They rushed over to where the other infected were feasting and they burrowed their way through to partake of the human-flesh meal.

"Oh my God," the reporter said before he gagged. The cameraman followed him as he doubled over, vomiting his stomach contents on the rooftop tar. The camera panned from the puking reporter back to the cannibalistic zombies below. A few seconds later, the screen flipped back to the anchorwoman in the news room who was speechless at first. She cleared her throat and looked around nervously at the others in the newsroom before making her statement.

"Ladies and gentlemen, I've been instructed once again to warn all Chicago citizens to please seek shelter away from the city. Military personnel are doing what they can to contain the situation, but until then, please take only what provisions you need and evacuate the city immediately. If you cannot evacuate, please barricade yourself in your home as securely as you can. NBC Channel Five News will keep you updated for as long as we can and let you know as soon as new developments come in, so stay tuned." The channel then went to the emergency broadcast message, signaling the loud siren and then reissuing the emergency evacuation alert.

Sarah's chest heaved furiously as she struggled to comprehend what she had just seen. Vincent walked over to her, grabbing her by the shoulders.

"Sarah, breathe, listen to my voice. We're going to be okay," he told her.

She nodded. "I'm fine…" she panted between ragged breaths. "But I saw them, Vincent. I saw them when they were so close to me! Oh my God, they moved so fast! I thought they were going to get me."

Seeing Sarah in her hysterical state, he knew she had been trying to hold herself together and stay focused, but watching the news footage triggered something in her. It triggered something in him as well. He knew it was fear, but maybe there was something else... was it hopelessness?

He pulled her close to him, holding her as tightly as he could. *God if I could take it all back, I would,* he thought. "I'm so sorry, baby. I'm so sorry."

"I've got to ask, how far away where they when you saw them?" Felicia asked, realizing that the creatures could have followed her into the building.

"When that happened, I was about five blocks away. I ran like hell to get home," Sarah said, still holding on to Vincent.

"Shit!" William cursed as he went to the window, looking down. "They're everywhere. I can't believe it's spread this fast in less than two hours."

"I don't supposed the CDC has an emergency protocol for zombies, do you?" Vincent asked.

"We're prepared for many various outbreak scenarios, but this shit takes the cake. I'm not going to lie to you. We've never dealt with anything like this before," William said.

"It's as if they're superhuman," Sarah said.

"They're definitely *not* human and *that* gives them the advantage," Felicia said. "Which is why I don't see why we're wasting time in this condo when we should be getting our asses on the roof!"

"I agree," Samantha said.

"What if we get trapped there before the helicopter comes?" Sarah asked. "At least here in the condo we have weapons.

"From what I've seen of those things, it won't matter where we're at. If we get caught by them, we're as good as dead,"

Samantha said.

"How are we going to seal the door?" William asked, looking around the condo for possible material.

"I've got my tool box," Vincent said, pointing toward the medium size box on the floor beside the closet. "William, help me take these doors down." He pointed to both the bedroom and hallway bathroom doors.

William nodded and the two men busied themselves removing the two doors.

"All right, we use these to barricade the door. Once we go up, we don't come down. By no means, is that understood?" Felicia asked as she eyed her companions.

"Understood," they said in surprising unison.

"Good." Felicia nodded curtly. "Let's gather everything."

She took the bag containing Vincent's research and hard drives. Samantha looked at the bag with the food. She left it, thinking they wouldn't need it once they were free of the city. At least she hoped they'd be able to get more. The research was what was important to them, so she took the laptop. Sarah took the duffel bag with their clothes and money inside it and Vincent's toolbox.

Vincent looked around. "Okay, do we have everything we need before we leave here?" he asked, checking over his companions. "We won't be able to come back."

The two men held both doors together.

Samantha huffed. "We have everything that's important. Let's get the hell out of h--"

The loud ear-piercing siren of the fire alarm cut her off and put them all on a brand new level of alert.

"Shit, let's go," William said, walking toward the door.

"The elevators are out of the question, how close are we to the roof?" Felicia asked.

"Not far, thank goodness," Vincent said as he led them to the emergency stairwell that led to the roof. It was located around the corner and down the hall. They ran past a few people in the hallway who looked to be as confused as they were terrified. The hallway wasn't as crowded as Vincent thought it would be. He knew a lot of the residents were outside probably fighting for their lives. He prayed those who left earlier made it out of the city alive although he didn't have much hope. They were most likely dead.

The group rushed past several people as they neared the exit stairway. Vincent's neighbor, Bruce grabbed his arm stopping him before he could reach the door.

"Where the fuck are you going?! You can't go down there, Vincent. Those…those things are down there! That's why I pulled the alarm! They've got us trapped up here. We've stopped the elevators and we're blocking off all the stairways," Bruce informed.

"I need to get to the roof, Bruce. After we leave, then by all means, seal this damn thing shut." Vincent snatched his arm away and gestured for the others to check the stairway.

"The rooftop? Why are you going up there?" Bruce's wife, Maria, asked as she kept pace.

"We don't have time for this Q and A. Let's go," Felicia growled as she pushed past them toward the door.

"Wait! If you open that door, those things can come in here," Bruce protested as he thrust himself in front of her path, blocking her.

"I don't hear anyone banging on the door yet, so get out of our way," Felicia demanded in a tone that was as vicious as the monsters they were running from. "I'm with the CDC and we need to make it to the roof."

She didn't have time to dally around with panicked individuals. They had their best chance of getting a cure in their company and getting to the rooftop was her only priority.

"Take us with you… if you have a plan, please take us with you," Bruce begged as he slowly removed himself from their path.

"Fine, just get the fuck out of the damn way!" Vincent fussed.

Bruce did them one better and opened the door for them. The group rushed through and made their way up the staircase. Down below them, they could hear the screams and cries of the building residents dying on the floors below. They could also hear the footsteps pounding on the cement staircase as those trying to flee found exits that weren't yet sealed.

Together, they made their way to the rooftop and they could tell they weren't alone. Several pairs of footsteps followed behind them as others from Vincent's floor witnessed them fleeing through the stairwell. They had no time to persuade them otherwise, the group continued up the three flights until they reached the top. Once everyone who had run to the rooftop was out of the stairwell, Vincent and William immediately began applying Liquid Nail glue along the edge of the door. It wasn't the best in the line of defense, but it was all he had at the moment.

"Hopefully, this will help secure it in place," Vincent said as he reached for his hammer.

"It's better than nothing," William agreed.

Together the two men began nailing the heavy wood doors into place in their best attempt to barricade the main rooftop door.

"Wait, what if other people need to make it up here for safety?" Maria asked, gesturing towards the door in panic.

"We can't risk that, Maria," Vincent said as he drove a thick nail into the wood with his hammer. "We have to trust that anyone below us will be safe enough by sealing off the exits and barricading themselves in their apartments."

"Exactly," William added, then placed another wood door panel across the steel door, holding it in place.

Maria started to protest. "But—"

"—Look, damn it! This isn't a full proof plan, but it's what we've got. It's all we've got!" Vincent interjected, finally losing his patience.

"Just try to stay calm. We're having a copter pick us up soon and we can't afford to be overtaken by infected people or panicked individuals clamoring for a way out," William said.

"Right now, the situation's too extreme to resort to anything but every man for himself," Felicia said as she pulled her cell phone from her purse.

Maria started to protest. "I just feel so bad."

"It is what it is. I wish that none of this was happening right now, I really do… you have no idea. But it's all about survival now. We have to get to someplace safe to try to figure out how to stop this," Vincent said.

"What do you know about what's going on?" Bruce asked.

William continued to hold the piece of wood in place as Vincent hammered away.

"Vincent, what do you know?" Bruce repeated with more assertiveness.

Vincent paused his life-saving activity long enough to answer the question. "I'm not just a doctor, Bruce… I'm a scientist. We all are. We need to get to the nearest research facility and as far away from ground zero as possible if we're going to figure out how to cure those people."

"Well, shit… why are you stopping? Here let me help." Bruce decided to leave it at that for now. More questions could be asked later. He walked over to the two men and reached into the tool box removing the spare hammer. He worked on one end while Vincent worked on the other.

"Where the hell is that helicopter at?" Vincent asked Felicia as he pounded away on a nail, driving it deeper into the wood.

"I was just thinking the same thing," she said as she dialed another number and waited. "Please put me through to Deputy Director Dwayne Wheaton, this is Dr. Felicia Anderson."

She knew she had an audience listening to her conversation and she had to be careful about what information she shared. The last thing she wanted to do was cause a panic among them.

"Mr. Wheaton, we need evacuation out of Chicago ASAP, what's the ETA on our 'copter?" There was a pause from Felicia and she frowned, lowering her voice to a whisper, she continued. "You know my recommendation, it's not pretty, but I think it's necessary. We need to neutralize Chicago before it spreads too far. But before we do that, we have to gather all of the data from the lab and at Dr. Philip Pierce's residence. I believe him when he says we need it. I don't want to take any chances… Oh, you better believe I followed protocol as best I could considering our predicament."

She shifted from one foot to the other as she monitored the chaos on the streets below. The few National Guard soldiers who were fighting so gallantly were finally overtaken on Columbus Street. The rabid zombies fell upon them with such speed and ferociousness, there were unable to defend themselves or the people who had been preparing for the annual Taste of Chicago food festival and were now trapped downtown. Several tents were knocked down and grills had been turned over as people tried to flee. They screamed as they climbed over each other struggling to get away from the zombies. Firefighters posted at Columbus and Michigan Avenue attempted to hold the frenzied horde back with the powerful blasts of water from their hoses, but it only slowed the zombies down. Police officers fired their guns, emptying clip after clip into the army of zombies as they pressed onward. The powerful force of water from the fire hoses shredded their skin, but they didn't seem to register the pain as they crawled forward.

"God, please help us." Felicia closed her eyes from the horror and gave a silent prayer before returning to her phone call. "Dr. Masterson insists the information is vital." She paused again. "No, sir, I wouldn't recommend us attempting to breach SciTech Labs at this point. The place may still be overrun. Not only that, we don't know how to kill these things yet. I have never seen anything like this before, at least not outside of a movie theater. The only scientific label I can come up with to describe what is going on is a damned zombie attack. You've seen the news, you've had to. You know what's happening down here. We need to vacate now. We've manage to barricade ourselves on a rooftop, but we have no idea how long it's going to hold up against these things. They're already in the building."

She turned around, looking at the remaining survivors stranded on the rooftop. "We're going to need a few more helicopters as well. We have a few residents with us who need to be rescued. Please send them as soon as you can." Felicia nodded. "Thank you, Sir. We'll be waiting." She was about to end her call when she put it back to her ear. "Yes, Sir? …We don't know if it's airborne or not. So far, it looks like the virus is spread through physical contact with the infected person's saliva or blood or both."

"Tell him that these things are strong and fast, he needs to know that," William said, wanting Felicia to relay the information.

She nodded. "There's more, from the information we've gathered, these beings are very strong, stronger than the average human and fast, too. The speed in which a person is infected once killed seems to..." She paused, placing her hand over the mouthpiece and looked at William. "How long do you think it was from the moment that soldier was eviscerated until the moment he rose as one of them?"

William shrugged one shoulder. "It was damn near instantaneous."

Felicia nodded again. "Dr. Wheaton, these things can infect a person within seconds after they've been killed."

"You better tell him that animals may be infected, too," Vincent suggested remembering Patient Zero was actually a primate.

"Animals can be infected, too. Not sure which ones, though." Felicia looked at Vincent who nodded. "Jesus H. Christ," she fumed, thinking about their ever increasing fucked up situation. "As for the time frame it takes for this virus to incubate inside a human who's still alive, it's still undetermined. I would predict this city and maybe this state will be overtaken within twenty-four to forty-eight hours unless we figure out our next move."

After a few more minutes of listening to Dr. Wheaton, she nodded again.

"Very well, Sir. We'll be waiting," Felicia said, ending her call. She slipped her cell phone back into her purse once she checked her battery life.

After hammering one more nail into place, the door was as secure as it was going to get and the group settled as comfortably as they could among the other panicked individuals, nine to be exact, making it a total of fourteen, while they waited for their helicopters.

"We should have left with Jim and Rosa," Martin Forrester said to his girlfriend who was sitting beside him, trembling.

"Don't be an idiot. This is Downtown Chicago. Traffic on any given normal day is asinine. Look at it now," Vincent said, gesturing toward Lake Shore Drive. "Go on; look at what's happening down there."

Martin frowned, but he did rise and walk toward the edge to look down below. Cars were bumper to bumper, many were abandoned and others still held their owners inside seeking the only refuge they could find at the moment. It wasn't helping them; the zombies broke through glass windows, pulling victims from their automobiles.

William joined the two men. "You did the only thing that's going to give you a fighting chance. Anyone stuck in that down there is as good as dead."

Martin gasped as he witnessed an attack. "My God, I can't believe this shit! It's like they're clamoring over one another to get to the people first." With his birds' eye view, he watched several of the infected people leaping and running toward the soldiers and police officers who were desperately trying to hold them off and save the people trapped inside their vehicles. Unfortunately, the bullets had no effect on their attackers.

Felicia walked over to the edge to look down. She huffed in agitation. "You're right, William. It would be suicide for anyone who's trying to make it out of here on foot *or* wheels. With this traffic not moving, it's going to make it easier for this virus to spread when more and more people are attacked."

Vincent watched the real-life nightmare take place. Just a short time ago, those very same people were having breakfast or going to work and school. Their day started off so normal, so safe and predictable. God, just how many lives was he responsible for ruining?

"What do we do now?" asked one of the women who had joined them in their rooftop retreat.

"Right now, we're safe. We just have to keep calm and wait for help to come—and it's coming—we are just going to have to be patient and quiet," Felicia said, trying her best to keep the crowd calm.

"Is it the Coast Guard?" one of the people asked.

"I don't care who they send as long as I can get off this fucking rooftop. I don't give a shit if it's the Goodyear blimp, I'm hopping on that bastard," Bruce stated. He put his arm around his wife and she shivered, more from the fear she felt than the cool summer breeze.

Vincent looked over the edge from his high vantage point and saw nothing but carnage for miles all around. Hundreds if not thousands of cars were in flames or overturned as they remained abandoned and stranded in the streets below. He strained his eyes to see more details, but to no avail. His condo building stood fifty-one stories high, it kept them far enough from the danger below for the time being, but that just meant they were sitting ducks.

"How long before the helicopter arrives?" Vincent asked.

"I don't know. They had to deploy a lot more helicopters throughout the state. I'm hoping it doesn't take long," Felicia said. "It's already taking longer than it should have. I'm starting to worry."

Both Felicia and Vincent turned towards the adjacent building as the sounds of more screams echoed in the air. Twelve frightened people spilled out of the roof-top exit door, some falling to their knees, while others ran to the farthest edge of the roof. Two took the time to slam the door shut behind them and blocked it as best they could with their bodies as the person who appeared to be the custodian locked it.

"Oh my God!" Felicia gasped as she watched them in their desperation.

The two men tried to keep the zombies from bursting through by combining their mass and strength against the door. Six other men and women joined them, adding extra weight. The others who were on the rooftop with Vincent joined him and Felicia, curious as to what they were looking at. They all watched as the people on the other rooftop struggled to keep the zombies away from them.

"Damn it! Where are those fucking helicopters?" Felicia fussed. She moved her glove aside and looked at her watch; then growled in frustration.

The people on the other rooftop jumped and screamed when the door shook on its hinges. Those who were sitting quickly moved away from the door, nearly to the edge of the roof. The door shook each time it was pounded on from the other side. Two of the people who were standing near the edge looked around seeing no other option but to jump from the twenty-five story building. The couple held onto each other as they stepped onto the ledge. Again the door vibrated, the metal denting with each thrust of powerful fists. The couple standing on the ledge was joined by three more people, thinking suicide would be the more preferable option to being eaten alive.

"Jesus Christ, they're going to break through!" Vincent's heart pounded in his chest so hard, he thought it would burst through his ribcage. He could feel the nausea rising along with the bile from his stomach and he swallowed hard to keep it down. Transfixed, his eyes stared forward as he remained helpless and terrified, unable to do anything for the people on the other rooftop.

Eyes remained glued to the others across the way as the door began to dent outward as the threat on the other side pushed its way through. The screams got louder and more frantic as the dents in the steel door grew larger and larger. The steel door ballooned outward and the lock broke as the doorknob fell to the floor. The screams reached a brand new pitch, turning into shrill cries as the monsters found their way through, overtaking their frightened prey with vicious speed and savagery. The first to die were the men who gallantly held the door closed as long as they could. They fell under their attackers, punching and kicking as hard as they could. The monsters tore into the men, ripping away flesh and other bloody bits. They reared their heads back as they swallowed their bounty before diving in for more.

Dozens of black-eyed zombies filled the rooftop overtaking the people within an instant. The first couple to take to the ledge managed to jump to their deaths before the zombies could attack them. The others weren't so lucky. They were snatched from the ledge, limbs separating from flesh with the force of the attack as they were yanked down towards the monsters.

Vincent and the others watched in shocked dismay and horror as the dead fed furiously and brutally on the living. The one thing they knew for certain was that they would be next if they weren't rescued in time. They stood there, silent as the grave, watching other humans being devoured. Bloody teeth bit through warm flesh, ripping chunks from struggling bodies. Limbs were torn and eaten with no regard for human life.

Vincent grabbed Sarah and pulled her down hoping the monsters didn't see him. He reached out, pulling on the pants and shirts of those next to him, bringing them down, too. Soon, they were all hiding behind the edge and peeking over.

"We're going to die just like them if we don't get off this fucking rooftop!" Maria screamed. Her chest heaved as her breathing increased.

"Baby, calm down, we have to stay calm," her husband whispered in her ear repeatedly as if trying to convince himself as much as her. His own voice wavered as he struggled to keep from going into shock. He'd seen the carnage on the television, but not with his own eyes and not so close to him. God, those things were in the building! They were going to be next, he just knew it. He began to wonder if their barricade was strong enough to keep those things back before they could be rescued.

"You need to find out the ETA of that helicopter, or that shit's going to happen to our asses," William told Felicia.

"I'm already on it." Felicia had pulled out her cell phone and was now dialing her agency. "Where are those helicopters?"

"They're on their way, Felicia. Just hang on and keep a cool he —"

"Don't tell me to stay calm, Dwayne. You're safe, we're not!"

"Fair enough, but how is panicking going to help your case?"

Felicia's lips pressed tightly together. Every part of her wanted to reach into the cell phone and grab Dwayne by his neck and choke the life out of him.

"I'm not panicking... " She said and withheld adding the word "*Asshole*" to the sentence. "... But I am very concerned. How much longer, we don't have a lot of time left."

"Five minutes, tops," Dwayne replied.

"Let's hope we'll live that long." She ended her call, not wanting to talk to him any longer. "Fucking prick," she cursed under her breath.

"Well?" Samantha asked.

"He said about five minutes. I half expected him to ask for a status update," Felicia said sarcastically.

Sarah turned to Vincent, nudging him. "If they only send one helicopter, do you think there will be enough room?" she asked in a hushed tone so only Vincent could hear.

"No, but let's pray that both helicopters will arrive soon and I'm hoping that's enough," Vincent whispered. "If it doesn't weigh ours down, I'm going to try to squeeze in Alex and Maria."

"In all honesty, Vincent, there won't be enough room for them, just us five," Felicia said, after overhearing Vincent's response.

Vincent turned to her. "Then please, God, let both helicopters get here at the same time. I fear all hell is going to break loose if only one arrives."

"I sent for what I could. Remember, the priority here is you and the information you know. We're not going to be able to save everyone in Chicago," Felicia looked around at the others. *Or maybe even everyone on this rooftop*, she thought to herself.

"What are you saying… t-that you're going to leave us here?" Maria asked, her voice quivering in her frantic state.

"I'm saying we weren't planning on bringing more people with us. If the helicopter has room, of course we'll take you. If both copters I asked for come, then hop on that one as soon as you can. But if it doesn't or you're not fast enough and there's no more room, then you'll have to secure yourself on this roof until more help arrives," Felicia whispered, purposely lowering her voice so that Maria would do the same to keep others from hearing their conversation.

"We won't last long if that happens," Maria said. Several tears rolled down her cheeks as she looked from Felicia to her husband, Bruce.

"You already know we've called for more reinforcements and the Coast Guard and the National Guard are already in route," Felicia said as reassuringly as she could. By the bug-eyed expression on Maria's face, she knew her words gave the woman and her male companion not one ounce of comfort.

"We should let everyone know to hang tight. That more help will be coming," Sarah said.

"We'll do no such thing," Felicia said, giving the other woman a stern stare.

"It will prevent a panic when they helicopters arrive. Once people see that there isn't going to be enough room..." Sarah frowned.

"We're not going to do that, Sarah. Telling them that some of them are going to be left behind isn't going to calm people down and make them rational. If anything it's going to cause more panic and turn this into an every-man-for-himself situation before help arrives. We're trying to survive here, I don't want to fight for my life with the people on this roof," Vincent informed.

Sarah thought about what he said. She didn't like it—not helping people in need was damn near an impossible thing for her to do—but she couldn't deny the logic in his statement. Reluctantly, she nodded.

"Good," Vincent said. Slowly, he rolled over onto his belly and peaked over the edge to monitor the people who had been attacked on the other rooftop. The other scientists did the same. The roof was covered in blood, guts, and scattered body parts in the aftermath of the feeding frenzy. Only one naked female zombie remained, feasting greedily on the internal organs of a headless female corpse.

"I can't watch anymore," Sarah gasped as she turned away, lying back onto the tar-covered roof. She sobbed uncontrollably knowing that hundreds, if not thousands, of people were dying horrible deaths at that very moment. She couldn't believe that only a few hours ago, the city had been thriving with people going about their normal day. Laughing, eating, working, driving, walking… living. *What the hell was going on?*

Felicia turned away from the lone zombie feeding, not wanting to draw attention to their rooftop location. She looked at William and Samantha. "Funny how five minutes can feel like forever, isn't it?" she commented.

"Funny isn't the word I'm thinking about." Vincent turned to Sarah. "Let me see your cell, I want to check on Richard and Linda."

"Oh my God, yes, please," Sarah handed him her cell.

Vincent called Richard and only got his voicemail. He hung up then called Linda's cell and she answered.

"Thank God I reached you, are you okay? What about Richard?" Vincent asked.

"We're both fine. By the grace of God, Richard made it out of SciTech before they could get him. I'm so grateful you're alive. What about Sarah?" Linda asked her voice full of concern.

"We're okay, too. Hold on, I'm putting you on speaker, Sarah's right here." Vincent pulled the cell from his ear and adjusted the setting. "Okay, we can both hear you now. Are you still in the city?"

"No, we're in Indiana now, but we're stuck in traffic. Richard thinks we need to get out and run, but I don't know."

Oh sweet Jesus, Sarah thought. She looked at Vincent and then at Felicia. The three of them shared the same fear. There was no solace in either decision the couple had. Either way, they could be doomed. Tears began to run down Sarah's cheeks and she wiped them with the back of her hand.

"Are you still there?" Linda asked.

"What did they say?" Richard asked in the background.

"They aren't saying anything, now I'm really worried," Linda replied.

"Ah, how far away from Chicago are you?" Vincent asked.

"None of that matters," Felicia interjected. "Hello, you don't know me, but my name is Dr. Felicia Anderson from the CDC. These creatures are extremely fast on foot and they are spreading their ranks far beyond the city limits. If you stay in your car, you will be overtaken by them. Your best bet is to find a secure shelter —a place with very little entrances and windows. Lock yourselves inside and stay quite. I have no idea how well these things can hear, but you don't want to make loud noises that can draw them to you. Hopefully, help will arrive soon, but you don't, and I repeat, don't want to be caught out in the open when these things start attacking."

Vincent was impressed with the female doctor. Her quick responses to everything thus far earned her his respect, even if she didn't need it or want it, she had it.

"I agree with her, Richard," Vincent chimed in. "Find someplace safe, please. I don't want to lose my best friends."

"We don't want to lose us either," Richard said. "All right, this traffic hasn't moved anywhere in almost an hour, we're outta here. Come on, baby."

"We'll call you back once we get somewhere safe. What about you? Where are you?" Linda asked.

"On the rooftop of our condo. A helicopter's coming to pick us up. Don't worry about us. Please, just go and be safe," Vincent urged.

"All right, bye," Linda said.

"See you later," Vincent said.

"See you soon," Sarah added.

Vincent clicked off the phone and gave it back to Sarah. "God, I pray that they'll be all right."

Sarah nodded.

"Can I ask a question?" Maria looked at the three CDC doctors. "What is it?" Felicia replied.

"Is the government going to bomb the city?" Maria whispered.

William nodded and answered the question, "It's the only way to contain the situation now. Destroy everything before it can spread any further than it already has."

"Wouldn't they do that as a last resort?" Sarah asked.

"Don't you think we're at our last resort?" William shot back. "Look around you. It's been less than two hours and the city is in complete chaos."

"Can you cure these people?" Sarah asked Vincent, looking at him with the innocent blue eyes he'd fallen in love with ten years ago.

He shook his head, running a finger over a furrowed brow. "Shit, I don't know, Sarah. I won't know if we can do anything until I get a combined look at my research and Dr. Pierce's. Even then, I still don't know."

"Truth be told, I don't think these people can be saved," William said. "Those things down there are dead—reanimated corpses. You can't cure that."

Vincent nodded. "I'm hoping I can cure someone who's infected, but still alive. Hopefully, I can reverse the effects of the virus before it turns them into one of those things."

"I hope so," Sarah said.

She jumped at the sound of glass shattering two stories beneath them. The shattered glass was followed by the terrified scream of someone who'd just jumped from their condo. The sound of his voice faded the further he fell until it was silenced indefinitely.

"Oh Jesus! Help us!" she prayed as she gripped Vincent's hands.

"God, please let this damn helicopter get here!" Felicia gave her own prayer, just one of many she's said since receiving that telephone call from Bryant. Whatever forced that person to jump to his death, they didn't want any part of it.

"I think this is our ride... at least I hope it is," William said, pointing to the two white helicopters flying their way.

The helicopters drew nearer, hovering over the rooftop. Their blades rotated furiously creating powerful gusts of wind that whipped up dust and particles around them. They had to shield their eyes as they rose to their feet, making room for the aircraft to land. When it did, the five of them quickly forced their way through the frenzied crowd to climb aboard. The others tried to push toward the helicopter's entrance, but armed soldiers held them at bay with the help of big guns and serious "I'll pull the trigger" expressions.

"You can't just leave us!" one of them cried.

"When we take off, the other helicopter can land and you can board it, this one is full," one of the soldiers screamed over the sound of rotating blades right before he closed the door. Soon, Vincent and the others could feel themselves rising into the air and the aircraft began to fly away from the building making room for the other helicopter to land.

"We got here as soon as we could under the circumstances," Dr. Darnell Powers addressed the group, shouting over the noise of the rotating blades of the helicopter as it lifted upward. "My name is Dr. Darnell Powers from the Illinois Department of Public Health."

"No need to apologize, I'm just glad you arrived when you did," Felicia replied then she introduced herself as she fastened her seat belt. The memory of those unfortunate souls who had taken refuge on a rooftop only to be killed and eaten before help could arrive still haunted her. She only hoped that wouldn't be the same fate for those they had to leave behind.

"What's the situation look like outside the city?" Vincent asked as he peered through the window toward his condo watching as the others began to fight amongst themselves for a space on the second helicopter. "Jesus..." he whispered to himself as he witnessed the scene from his vantage point.

The soldiers on the helicopter fired several bullets towards the crowd to keep them back and to give them enough time to slam the door. In a rush, the aircraft lifted with the ones they could take and began to follow Vincent's.

"Pure mayhem," Dr. Powers replied, bringing everyone's attention towards him. "These things are advancing and multiplying faster than the police and military forces can stop them. It just seems to take a single fatal wound from one bite to turn a normal human into one of those things out there." He shook his head in dismay with a low grumble. He looked at Felicia. "You can remove your helmets. We know enough about this virus to know it's not airborne."

"You've tested the air?" Felicia questioned.

Dr. Powers nodded. "We did. I can't tell you how relieved I was to be able to rule that out, at least."

"That's good enough for me. This thing was getting hot as hell," William said as he began removing his helmet. Sam and Felicia did the same, taking in huge gulps of fresh air.

Dr. Power looked at Vincent. "I've been briefed on you, Dr. Masterson, but I'm sure I don't know everything. For instance, just what in the hell were you working on?"

Vincent frowned as he stared down at the carnage below—the horrific growing aftermath of their "experiment toward the human advancement in bioengineering." That was just one of many smoke-up-the-ass lines the General had tossed at him when he asked about the project.

"We created something that I can't explain, Doctor. I'm going to do my best to find a cure. I don't know how successful I'll be with that, and I don't know how long it's going to take me. Most of my research and all of the current data is still located at SciTech labs, as I explained to your colleagues," Vincent answered.

"I'm well aware of that and that wasn't my question. What were you working on?" Dr. Powers repeated.

"In all honesty, Doctor… I don't really know. We were given a sample of some foreign substance. I'd never seen anything like it in my life. It mimicked blood in its consistency and color. It even had several variations of white and red cells but no definitive genetic code."

Vincent went on to explain what their job was regarding the sample—what SciTech labs was hired to do. "In the end, we had a breakthrough. One of our apes took to the injection with successful results… but the other, the one that was dying, its health only worsened. When it finally died, it didn't stay that way."

"Was the sample blood?" Dr. Powers asked.

"This helicopter was big enough to take a few more people,"

Sarah inadvertently interrupted after inspecting the extra room they had.

"Come again?" Dr. Powers asked, one eyebrow rising inquisitively.

"Oh, um, well, I'm just seeing that we had more room to bring more people with us. Why did your soldiers slam the door in their faces?" Sarah asked.

Dr. Powers sighed. "We were instructed to pick up a Mrs. Pierce and her two children then return to base. We left enough room to complete that task. Don't worry Mrs.—" He looked at her imploringly.

"Oh, it's Miss Freeman." She looked at Vincent, taking his hand into hers. "For now, it's just Miss Freeman."

"Touching," Dr. Powers returned his attention back to Vincent. "Now, back to my question?"

Sarah pouted, her top lip curling into a slight sneer at the castoff comment the other man gave her. Vincent squeezed her hand gently before lifting it to his lips for a tender kiss. His tone was curt when he responded to the doctor, but he held his rising temper in check. Now was not the time to get into an overprotective cock fight.

"About the sample, if it was blood, it wasn't any type of blood I'd ever seen. I don't know for certain what it was, but the biological properties that it contained were phenomenal. For instance, right before everything went to hell in a hand basket, we did manage to record the successful test subject's vitals. There was a spike in its heart rate and its brain activity increased showing significant cognitive response," Vincent said.

"So the test subject showed signs of heightened intelligence and an adrenaline level spike?" Dr. Powers looked at him for confirmation.

"Exactly, it was stronger and when injured, it healed instantaneously. It's what the government wanted. The project was a success. Unfortunately, I wasn't the one who made the breakthrough and the person who did… is one of those things down there."

Vincent's eyes studied the destruction below. Glass and splinters of wood littered the fronts of stores and restaurants that had had their windows and doors busted in. Dozens of buildings and skyscrapers were on fire as a failed result of the soldiers' attempt to gain control over the savage melee.

The worst of what he saw were the mutilated remains of the innocent people that had been gorged upon by what he could only label as *zombies*. But what disturbed him most was to see that the bodies were still moving, looking for other people to eat. They were missing limbs. Some were ripped in half, their entrails dragging along the pavement behind them leaving bloody trails slick with internal gore and bits of shredded organs they no longer seemed to need. There was no explanation for why they could still move. "Ungodly" was the best word Vincent could think of to describe the nightmarish sight.

"That's why it's so important we get to Clair, Philip's wife, and his research," Vincent said.

Dr. Powers studied him carefully. He was amazed that the scientist managed to escape the facility when so many others didn't. Needless to say, he was suspicious. "We'll be going back into SciTech Labs—"

"The fuck I am! Shit!" Vincent blurted out, inadvertently cutting the other man off. "Downtown Chicago is overrun with those fucking things. I'm not going back in there! I'm sorry. I just can't. Not until we figure out a way to stop them—what the fuck!" Vincent pressed himself up against the glass to gain a better view of what caught his eye. Others followed suit, looking around trying to locate what he'd seen.

"What? What is it?" Sarah asked.

"Oh my God, what the fuck is that?!" Vincent asked, pointing to a figure moving at a fast speed up the side of the building.

"Jesus Christ, I haven't seen those things do that before," Dr. Powers' voice came out in a breathless gasp as he watched in stunned horror at a being ascending the John Hancock building, a gigantic skyscraper towering over many other buildings in the city's downtown area. This being took each story with speed and effortlessness until it had quickly reached the top.

"Oh God, are you seeing this shit?" Vincent asked the others.

"Hell yeah, what the fuck is it doing?" William asked, dropping his usual calm and professional demeanor in his sudden state of shock. He was staring hard at the creature having squeezed himself in between Vincent and Sarah to gain a better view.

"I don't know, but it's watching us," Dr. Powers said, observing the creature. "It doesn't look like the rest of those things down there and I haven't seen one of them climb a building... at least not yet."

The creature's eyes followed their helicopter before it turned toward the second helicopter that was closer. Vincent stared hard at the creature. There was something about him. The color of his hair, the hotel uniform he was wearing... it looked so familiar.

"Oh my God, I think I recognize him," Vincent gasped.

"Who is he and what the hell is he doing?" Felicia watched as the creature lowered himself, its eyes fixed upon the second helicopter. "Please tell me it's not going to—"

They all screamed as the creature leapt high into the air, propelling himself from the roof of the Hancock Center onto the second helicopter, hooking his arm around the one of the landing skids. From their viewpoint, Vincent and the others saw the passengers in the helicopter scream as the aircraft listed slightly from the extra and unwanted weight. The creature wrapped one leg on the landing skid and pulled himself upward. He took hold of the door's handle and with a great show of strength, wrenched the door from it hinges, flinging it into the air.

"Oh my God!" Sarah shrieked, speaking for the others who are almost speechless save a few surprised and terrified gasps.

The creature wasted no time climbing into the helicopter and attacking the passengers, all of whom were Vincent and Sarah's neighbors and friends. He buried fangs deep into the throats of several victims, slurping greedily as he ripped open jugulars. Blood splattered the windows, leaving arterial sprays in cross-cross patterns. The helicopter pilot tilted the aircraft sideways as if trying to toss the creature out. Two bloodied and mangled corpses tumbled out the open doorway, falling thousands of feet to the pavement.

Vincent's own helicopter's speed increased putting a considerable distance between them and the doomed helicopter. Still, they were able to see the last attempts of the pilot's struggles to stay alive. The helicopter twisted and turned. Its tail rotator slammed into another skyscraper damaging the blades and shattering several windows sending glass raining down on the zombies and their terrified victims below. Soon, the helicopter was out of control, spiraling downward until it crashed into street. The blades ripped into the pavement as they shredded and spun wildly. Before they lost complete sight of the helicopter, they managed to see the creature emerge from the mangled debris. He stood in front of it calmly. Then right before their eyes, he ran faster than any human could manage.

"Did you see that?" Vincent looked around bug-eyed at the others hoping he wasn't the only one who witnessed the inhuman feat.

"I saw what you saw, that thing took down an entire helicopter and then damn near vanished," William said. He turned towards Felicia. "Either these things are mutating or that was something else altogether."

"I really don't know," Felicia said in a dazed tone. She was still in shock from what she'd seen. "Dr. Masterson, you said you knew him, where did you see him before?"

"Shit... I... I saw him at the hotel, at least I think it was him, I couldn't tell. He just looked familiar," Vincent replied, his words coming out shaky and uncertain. "He looked like one of the employees I'd spoken to after I got off the phone with you."

"What the hell is going on?" Felicia presented the question to no one in particular.

"All I know is that this situation just keeps getting worse. We just lost a 'copter full of civilians and soldiers. You better start fucking talking, Doctor!" interjected one of the uniformed soldiers, who had been silent up until this point. He grabbed Vincent by his collar, yanking him from his seat and pulling him closer.

"Get your fucking hands off me!" Vincent growled, pushing himself back from the soldier.

The other man released his grip on Vincent clothes, but kept his eyes intently on him. "What the fuck was that down there?"

"How the hell should I know?" Vincent yelled. "I've never seen any shit like that before!"

"We've got to figure out what that thing was and fast. It leaped at least fifty yards into the air to attack that helicopter," Samantha said, her gaze shifting from person to person.

Dr. Power spoke up, "Those other things, they're fast and strong as hell, especially as a group... but they stay grounded." He looked at Vincent. "You said this is the same guy you met earlier... did he seem normal to you?"

"Yes. Assuming it was him, he seemed really freaked out by what I was telling him. He must have been bitten, but why is he different from those other zombies?" Vincent was completely perplexed.

"That's something else we're going to have to get to the bottom of. We need to know if this virus is mutating or if it's something else out there attacking people," Dr. Powers said.

"God, help us," Sarah said.

"We're going to have to go into SciTech Labs," the angry soldier said.

"Excuse me, but who are you?" Vincent asked in a huff. His own adrenaline levels were spiked and he was a bit on edge. Still, he felt he should at least get that much of an introduction since the other man seem to have no problem putting his hands on him.

"Sgt. Hicks and those were my men who went down with that helicopter thanks to your little freak experiment," Hicks offered with a sizable measure of scorn.

The disdain in his tone wasn't lost on Vincent, but he'd be damned if he took all of the blame for what was happening. If the government hadn't wanted their damned super-soldiers none of this would be happening.

"Look I know you're looking for someone to blame and me

being the closest target, I guess I'll do. But I've got news for you, buddy. This didn't start with me. I'm hoping I can end it. I agree that we need to get into my lab, but now is not the time. The city is too overrun," Vincent said.

Especially if the shit we just saw is out there, too, he thought. A part of him was scared shitless at the prospect of returning to his lab. The very thought of being in the same area with one of the infected filled him with terror. He imagined his very own gory demise if he were to foolishly venture back into the lab. Even with an army, he didn't think he'd ever survive—or at least come out still human. The other part knew he was right about being better prepared.

"I was actually getting to that point before you interrupted me," Dr. Powers said grimly to Vincent. "We're in the process of forming an elite squad to go back into SciTech and retrieve the data, but they're going to need your help."

"They want me to go with them?" Vincent asked with both eyebrows rising high on his forehead.

"No. That's a risk we can't take. So relax for now, Dr. Masterson," Dr. Powers said. "You'll be guiding the team from the IDPH headquarters in Springfield."

"Oh, okay," Vincent said with a nod. He leaned over, looking out the window.

"I'm sorry," he whispered to those dying down below.

Collectively they all looked out of the widows watching as humans fled their traffic-jammed automobiles in search of safety as more zombies overtook those who were encumbered or simply not fast enough to get away.

"Sweet Jesus! These things attack like a swarm of locusts!" Sarah watched wide-eyed and in complete shock as she observed the hoard of running zombies attacking the people. The speed and ferociousness with which they killed and fed was as terrifying as it was extraordinary. It was unbearable for her to witness, knowing that people were dead and dying horrible deaths and not knowing how or why it was happening. Tears begin to fall from her eyes as she watched and listened to the people screaming and waving at their helicopter, begging for them to save them. There was nothing she could do. There was no comfort or help she could give them.

Vincent turned away from the scene, unable to face the result of his experiment. He wondered how many people were able to find shelter. How many were hiding somewhere waiting to be saved? How many manage to make it out of the city before it became overrun like his best friends? He looked at his companions, Sgt. Hicks and the other soldiers' glares were accusatory and angry. The others' expressions were filled with so many emotions.

However, it wasn't until he looked at his fiancée and saw her pain that it all hit him again. His earlier attempt as sharing the blame didn't seem justified now. How could he disagree with them? Even though he wasn't working alone—even though it wasn't him who had initiated the experiment—he had still played a huge part in what would be the total decimation of human existence if they didn't find a solution. That thought alone filled him with such dread, anger, hopelessness, and, above all, guilt.

"Jesus H. Christ, if we don't gain some sort of control now, at this rate, the entire North and South American continents will be taken over in a matter of days," William said.

"We have to make sure we keep the outbreak contained to this area at least. We really can't let this virus spread past the state let alone overseas," Felicia said.

"From what I can see, the virus attacks the human body so quickly an infected person won't have a chance to board an airplane before turning into one of them," Samantha stated.

Vincent's head shot toward her. "We don't really know that for certain, do we?"

"What?" Samantha looked at him.

"I think he means, we really don't have any case studies to prove that the virus can transform an infected person in a matter of minutes," Felicia clarified. "Depending on how badly the victim was injured, it could take anywhere from a few minutes to hours for them to change."

"That's exactly my point," Vincent said. "As a matter of fact, we don't even know if an injured person would turn—"

"—Oh, I'm almost certain they'll turn, all right," Dr. Powers stated. "We received cell phone footage of someone who'd been bitten on the shoulder. Somehow he managed to get away. He stated the he'd been bitten within the first hour since the outbreak was reported. The wound immediately—"

"—became infected." Vincent finished his sentence, remembering Dr. Henrick's condition.

Dr. Powers nodded. "He'd gone to St. Noel's hospital."

"Was the injury life-threatening?" Samantha asked.

"His was, yes," Dr. Powers answered.

"So, we still have a discrepancy in time. Critical injuries versus non-critical injuries," Felicia pointed out.

Vincent moaned slightly as he held his stomach. He swallowed hard as he fought the wave of nausea the movement from the helicopter induced. Licking his lips, moistening them, he attempted to explain.

"You going to be okay?" William asked.

"I hope so. I'm not used to riding in a helicopter," Vincent said.

"We need to have the FAA ground all flights. There are hundreds, if not thousands of people in and out of airports every day. Those numbers have probably tripled by now. One infected person… Oh my God. We need to check the status of Midway and O'Hare airports," Felicia said.

"Not only that, but we need to check the trains, Amtrak in particular," William said.

Dr. Powers scrolled through the numerous text messages he'd received in the last two hours. "We were getting reports about the national transportation system on the way to retrieve you. We're already far too late. Police were unsuccessful maintaining order at Union Station, Greyhound… hell, even all of the CTA train stations downtown and near the north side were under attack. There have been several derailments reported by Metra and the CTA. By this time, I can only image it's spread to the nearest suburbs surrounding the Chicago area. It's spreading faster than we can contain it."

"I know for a fact they're gotten as far as Skokie," Vincent said, remembering Clair's predicament.

"What about the hospitals?" Sarah asked.

"The reports we were getting aren't good," Dr. Powers said. "Rush Hospital is currently under attack, we don't know if anyone was able to make it out. Stroger was also attacked. I fear that might be the future of every hospital until we figure out a cure and how to kill these damn things."

Sarah wiped the tears from her eyes and cheeks. "What are we going to do?"

Secretly, Vincent was tired of hearing that question mainly because he didn't have an answer. All he could think of was surviving somehow, some way. Plan A was to evacuate Chicago. Plan B was to get somewhere far away from the danger zone. Hell if he knew what Plan C was going to be.

"Vincent, do you have a plan?" Sarah asked, putting him in broad view of everyone's theoretical spotlight.

Shit, not now, he thought. He opened his mouth to give her some kind of response, but Felicia spoke first.

"Getting into SciTech Labs is our next plan of action," she said. "Any update on that team, has it been assembled yet?" Felicia asked.

"I'm still waiting to hear back. With everything that's happening, it hasn't been easy arranging a team. The military has been doing emergency evacuations in other states and cities near Illinois in case we can't contain the outbreak to this city."

"How far are we from Clare's house?" Vincent asked.

"We'll be there shortly," Dr. Powell affirmed.

"Good." Vincent nodded as he looked out of the window. He had to get to Philip's research. It was their only hope.

Chapter Five

Aaron ran past several zombies who were far too busy ripping into the flesh of their victims to bother with him, especially since he was moving far too fast for them to catch him. Having been bitten twice by those damn things trying to get to Cassian, he was making sure he avoided them at all cost. Bypassing the elevator that was covered in bloody hand prints, he chose the staircase. He opened the door to a horrific sight; more zombies were devouring the residents who didn't make it out of the building in time. He leaped pass them for several floors, racing up the stairs one flight at a time until he reached the luxury penthouse condominium on the 89th level.

He pulled the door behind him, jamming it in the frame in an attempt to keep the zombies off that floor. He walked to each elevator and punched through the panels, shorting it out and sending tiny sparks flying from the damaged portal. Satisfied that he'd barricaded the floor, at least long enough to do what needed to be done, he turned, heading towards the main penthouse—his destination. He banged on the door repeatedly until the human inside answered.

***

Robert had been enjoying his Blu-ray box set of the newest season of the Knights of the Darkness Chronicles when he was interrupted by the obnoxious banging on the front door. He placed his bowl of cereal on the table and climbed off the sofa. After taking a glance at the security camera, he pushed the intercom button.

"Who are you and what do you want?" he asked with more attitude than was necessary. "You look like hell, by the way."

"My name is Aaron Young and I have to see the Master. Something's going on, something horrible and he needs to know," he shouted through the door. "Please let me in!"

"No can do. I'm not in the habit of letting strange bloody vamps into my Master's lair," Robert replied.

"Listen to me, you human fuck—"

"Whoa, whoa, you don't talk to me that way. I'm not just any human—"

"You're a Feeder like the rest of them, you just happened to be a little higher on the food chain. But I guarantee you this, if you don't let me in to warn the Master—"

Robert interrupted. "What will you do? You can't touch me."

Aaron inhaled deeply as he fought to keep his calm. With a slow and steady inhale and exhale, he continued. "Please, I mean the Master no harm. But you have to let me in. It's really important. Have you seen what the fuck's going on outside?"

Robert looked around the condo towards the windows. All he saw was an amazing view of the Chicago skyline from the Trump Towers. *What the hell was this guy talking about?* Okay, so there seemed to be a few more helicopters flying around the city than normal. *Yeah, that was weird*, he thought.

"You have my attention."

"Good, have you seen the news?" Aaron asked him, finally happy to be making some sort of progress.

"No, can't say that I have. Look, just tell me what the hell's going on."

"Zombies are attacking the city and they're in the lower levels of this building. We have to get the hell out of here. I've done what I can to protect this floor, but I don't think it will hold up." Aaron stared forward at the thick, heavily enforced wooden door, wishing he was strong enough to knock it down instead of having to yield to the weak human who was currently keeping him at bay and in a dangerous predicament. He could hear the human laughing on the other side of the door and it made him want to rip his throat out.

"Listen damn it! I'm not lying. Look at me!"

He took several steps backwards hoping the camera would be able to capture his appearance. His clothes were soaked in the blood of the people he'd slaughtered in the hotel and on the helicopter. His face was covered in it. His fingers still had bits of flesh clinging to them. He hoped this would convince the servant to let him in or at least check out his story.

"Do you see?"

Robert was speechless as he gazed at the camera. He had noticed the blood on the vampire's face, but he had no idea he'd be covered in it from head to toe. It was rare for vampires to have an appetite for human blood until the sun set. This vampire had obviously gorged himself in human victims before noon and had made a mess of himself in doing so.

"What happened?" Robert asked, this time in a more serious tone.

"I don't know. I got bit twice by those things out there. The next thing I vaguely remember is blood. Wanting it, needing it and not getting enough of it. Eventually the haze faded and I came back to my senses and I wasn't hungry anymore. I was trying to get here to warn the Master when it happened again. I'm okay now, though," Aaron explained it as best he could.

"If something out there bit you, then you've got to understand that I can't let you in here. I can't risk the Master being hurt."

"I said I'm okay," Aaron argued.

"That may be, but if you really care about the Master, then you should understand my position." Robert held fast.

In spite of how inconvenient it was since he didn't like being exposed to the danger that was on the other side of that stairway door, he had to admit the human was right. His sanctuary would have to wait. He didn't know if he was still infected or not and he didn't want to hurt his Master.

"Fine. I'll stay out here, but you have to go to him, he needs to know," Aaron warned.

"Yeah, that we can agree on. I'll be back." Robert walked away from the door back toward his television. He turned off the Blu-Ray player and turned on the news for the first time that day. The bloody vampire was right. Immediately, footage of the carnage that was going on right outside was displayed over the large seventy-two inch flat screen LCD television. Amateur video footage captured a horde of zombies converging on a group of policemen who were emptying every clip they had into the unstoppable force coming at them but to no avail.

"Holy shit!" Robert gasped as he stepped away from the screen as if the zombies would come through. It was all true, but how could it be? Zombies didn't exist. But of course, people said the same thing about vampires and he knew for a fact that wasn't true. He tossed the remote control on the sofa and ran towards the window, looking down instead of up. There he saw it—the fires, the clogged traffic and the many emergency vehicles cluttering dozens of streets. From his position high above the city, he could run to every side of the condo and get a damn good view of Chicago and that's exactly what he did. Everywhere he looked, he saw the same scene—death and more death.

How in the hell could I not know this was happening, he thought. "Because you were too busy watching your series." he answered his own question out loud. That explained how the news didn't take over his programming. As fast as he could, he ran to the Master's bedroom. Robert knocked gently at first and when he didn't get a response, he began to bang on the door in earnest.

Seconds later, the door swung open faster than Robert could prepare for and a hand dealt a powerful blow to his chest, knocking him backward to the ground. His back slammed into the wall as the air left his lungs in a painful rush. He looked up at the vampire who was glaring down at him.

"You better have a good reason for disturbing me." Cassian's eyes bored into the human's, demanding an answer.

Robert rubbed the sore spot on his chest as he nodded. "Master, we have to get out of the city. It's under attack by zombies."

Cassian's expression grew more menacing, his eyes darkening as his lips curled into a frown. "I am not in the mood for games, Robert or pranks, as you well know."

Robert shook his head. "As I'm not one to play them on you, Master. It's true. I've seen it on the news. I've also seen that there's something terrible happening with my own eyes. We have to get out of here. There's a vampire out there who told me about it," he pointed down the hallway leading to the living room area.

Cassian gave his human one last suspicious look before stepping past him. He made his way into the living room and focused on the television screen that was still playing live video of the zombies attacking. Like Robert, he too walked toward the windows and looked down. He saw the same disaster scene that had prompted the human to bang madly on his door. Not only that, but he could smell blood, lots of it and from different people just outside of his front door. He walked over to the security monitor and glanced at the young vampire covered in blood who stood nervously outside.

"Robert," he called the human to him.

"Yes, Master?" Robert answered when he rounded the corner.

"Is this the vampire who warned you?"

"Yes, Master. But I didn't want to let him in because he told me he'd been bitten twice by those things and turned all rabid."

Cassian turned sharply, both eyebrows raised in unconcealed shock. "What?"

"He might be infected still, Master. I didn't think it was safe to let him in," Robert said in his defense. He was hoping that expression on his master's face wasn't for him and his decision. He was just doing was he was supposed to do—protect the Master at all costs.

"How could he have been infected? I've never known any diseases or virus that could harm us," Cassian wondered aloud. He returned his gaze back to the monitor. He needed to know more and he knew he had to take a chance eventually if he was going to save his species. He opened the door and looked at the frightened vampire who was now going to one knee before him.

"Master," Aaron, said with an audible reverence to his tone.

"Rise and come inside," Cassian said, stepping away from the door to allow the vampire entry.

Aaron walked into the Master's lair, closing the door behind him. He looked around the condo in sheer wonderment, taking in the beautiful furnishings, ancient and exotic artwork and sculptures. He had overheard stories from other vampires higher up the chain of command about the Master's home, but he never imagined it being this breathtaking.

"Tell me what happened," Cassian demanded, getting right to the point.

Aaron snapped out of his awestruck state at the strict tone of his Master's voice.

He nodded curtly. "I was at work when it all went down. This guy comes in all bloody wearing one of those bio-suits. He asks to use the phone, so I let him. He calls the CDC and tells them that there's been an outbreak at SciTech Labs and that we need to evacuate the city. Before he leaves, he tells us to evacuate the hotel. Of course my boss didn't want to do that. I decided to lock the hotel doors and just when the guests start to panic we see people running down the street through the windows and glass doors. I knew they were running from something. I didn't have your number to call you, so I was going to come here. That's when we saw those people get attacked. It happened so fast. Before I knew it, they came busting through the windows and attacking all of the guests inside the hotel. I tried to kill one. I stabbed it in the chest with a letter opener, but it didn't even slow the damn thing down. We tussled for a bit then I managed to fling him from me, but then more of them began to attack me. One bit my arm..." He pointed to the spot on his arm where he'd been attacked. The wound had healed already, so there was no mark or scar for Cassian to see.

"Then what happened after it bit you?" Cassian asked.

"That's when everything just went black. Then I saw red. It was all just a blur. All I felt was this intense hunger. I've never felt the need for blood that strongly in my life, not even after I was first turned. After the *First Rise*, even that couldn't compare. It was like the *First Rise* times ten. I have no idea how many people I killed. Then I ran as fast as I could to get here when I was attacked again. It's like they came at me from all angles. I felt the same blackout and bloodlust but after I took out this helicopter full of passengers, I instantly began to feel normal again. The hunger went away like that." He snapped two fingers together for effect.

Cassian was contemplating everything the young vampire was telling him. He was worried, whatever was affecting the humans down there—turning them into those things could do the same thing to them. What made it worse was that they were inhuman. His people would become an even bigger threat to the humans if infected. He turned toward his human servant. "Contact my lieutenants. We need to take action."

"There's something else, Master," Aaron began.

"Speak." Cassian stared hard at the younger vampire.

"I know how to kill these things. At least one way. Remove their heads from their body. The same way you'd do with a vampire," Aaron informed. "I had to take out some of them like that on the way here."

"Interesting," Cassian mused. He walked over to a large, ancient broadsword sitting on display on his sidebar. He ran a finger along the hilt fondly. "You've done well giving me this information."

"Thank you, Master. Please, forgive me, but we really need to get the fuck out of this city," Aaron politely suggested as best he could considering the stress he was under. "It's a fuckin— it's a war zone down there and the government is telling all of the citizens to evacuate."

Cassian turned, facing Aaron. "We will, but first we need to figure out exactly what's going on. This started at SciTech Labs, you say?"

"That's what the guy said," Aaron said.

Cassian huffed in annoyance. "Find out if that's true, now."

Robert ran towards the computer, turning it on. Aaron pulled out his cell phone and began searching the net for information. Almost at the same time, both men were offering him answers.

"One at a time," Cassian commanded. "Robert, tell me."

"Master, there are several reports that state SciTech Labs was the first to be attacked," Robert said.

"I'm getting the same information. Apparently, people think

they were working on some kind of experiment and it went wrong. At least that's what some so-called experts are saying on CNN," Aaron offered.

"SciTech Labs? What kind of facility is this and where can I find it?" Cassian looked at both men. They got the hint and turned back to their respective screens searching for the information.

"SciTech Labs is a research facility located downtown." Aaron retrieved the information first, giving Cassian the address. "They're supposed to be all into organic medicines and studying new environmental elements, whatever the fuck that means," he said.

"Well ain't shit 'organic' about those things down there," Robert quipped.

"About them," Aaron looked at Cassian. "Master, they're in this building and they'll be making their way up here soon enough. I've barricaded the doors on the way up here as best I could and damaged the elevators, but I don't know how long that's going to hold them off since they're in the stairwell."

Cassian nodded. "You did well." He turned back to Robert. "My lieutenants, now."

The order was not to be ignored or delayed any longer and Robert immediately pulled out his cellphone and began making calls to the human servants of the Master's right-hand vampires. He woke up two servants via three-way calling, who happened to be sleeping on the job. He gave them the information then ended the call. While flipping through the contact list, his cell began to ring. It was the last servant he was about to call.

"Please tell me you know what's going on?" He asked by way of greeting.

"Do you? 'Cause I don't. I just know we need to leave," Veronica said.

"The Master wants all of his lieutenants with him, now."

"I figured as much, we're actually on our way. The door was a bit jammed, but we got it open."

"Wait, jam it again. Those things are in the building and we don't want them to get to this floor, at least not easily."

"Already ahead of you," Veronica said. "Open the door, we're outside."

Robert raced to the door and with a quick glance at the monitor, he opened it. Two tall identical twin vampires walked past him into the condo followed by a petite human female. Well, she was petite in stature, but everything else on her came with double servings. It was no wonder the twins had taken to the tiny beauty. That's what they were known as, The Twins, Alexis and Alexias. Upon first meeting them several years ago, Robert had had a good chuckle at the lack of creativity their parents had when naming them. Still, they were two of Cassian's most viscous and ruthless vampires and two of his most loyal.

"Master," the twins greeted in unison as if rehearsed.

Cassian stood by the window watching the streets below. He didn't turn around to address them, he just spoke. "I'm not going to waste time. I want you to organize the vampire Lords of my territory powerful enough to take flight and have them gather as many humans of importance as they can. Make sure the humans are uninfected by this disease. Since we are susceptible as well, I don't want us to take any unnecessary risks."

Alexis frowned, his eyebrows knitting slightly. "We are susceptible? Wait... 'Of importance', Master? Who do you have in mind?"

Cassian sighed. "If you are bitten, you will turn into one of those things down there, killing blindly to feed your bloodlust. It's something we can not risk, especially not a vampire of your stature. Now, regarding the humans, we'll need to save those who can help remedy this situation. We're going to need scientists, doctors, soldiers... people who can help us defend and protect our interests."

"But if they try to fly them out of the city, they'll get shot down, no doubt," Aaron said. "Only authorized aircraft have been cleared to fly."

"How stupid are you?" Alexias tossed the insult at Aaron.

"What?" Aaron asked, frowning. He was still confused but now he was also humiliated and pissed.

"Surely, you didn't think he meant we'd use an airplane to fly? You must be extremely young," Alexias commented with a cocked brow.

"I'm aware of the standard human protocol in the case of emergency, Aaron." Cassian looked at the young vampire. "A few of my vampires will be slightly inconvenienced, but they are strong enough to take flight during the day."

"Holy shit," Aaron gasped under his breath.

He had heard rumors about the ancient vampires, the ones who held high positions under the Master, but he had no idea they were that powerful during the day. He could only imagine how powerful they would become once the sun set.

"They are simply superior beings, even to you," Cassian said, his tone as arrogant as the smirk that followed. He had read the young vampire's mind and knew he wished to be held in high regard. In fact, he now knew the young vampire went to his club the night before, looking for him dressed in the best he could afford on his hotel salary. He wanted to be one of his Elite. What better way to keep an inferior being in their position than to remind them of where they stood in your eyes?

He turned toward the Twins. "You have your orders."

"As you wish, Master. May I ask where are we taking them?" Alexias inquired.

Before Cassian could reply, there was another knock on the door. Robert checked the monitor then he let the other lieutenants and their human servants inside the condo. Chloe entered trailed by her human companion, Patrick. After her was Cassian's second in command, the vampire strongest to take over in the event of his death, Sajan. His human servant, Nicole followed behind him. She gave Cassian and the other vampires a bow in show of respect and subservience.

"Did you see if those things have gotten any closer?" Aaron asked apprehensively. He had never been so close to vampire royalty—that's what they were considered. The Master and his lieutenants lived in the tallest building in the city in the most luxurious condos. It was well known that Cassian owned the condos they resided in. He hoped that his efforts would one day place him in an elevated position among the Elite. Hell, he'd even accept being considered for the position of a lord. Lords were the lowest ranking of the vampire royalty, but it would put him one step closer to where he wanted to be.

The other vampires and their humans ignored Aaron's question, their gazes were concentrated solely on Cassian. Their Master turned around, looking at them.

"Well, did they?" he asked, bringing focus to Aaron's question.

Chloe nodded. "I did inspect the stairway and heard them attacking humans on the fortieth floor. They'll be on this floor soon."

"I see," Cassian said, turning back to address Alexias' earlier question. "Once you gather them, take them to St. Louis."

"Gather what?" Chloe asked.

"Not what, who. We're to gather important people in significant positions," Alexis answered.

"Like scientists and doctors?" Chloe pointed out.

"Exactly." Alexias nodded.

Sajan whistled. "Concerning St. Louis, Cassian, is he expecting us?"

"He will be," Cassian replied with utmost certainly in his tone.

"Shouldn't we make sure? I don't want to land in his territory only to find out I'm not welcome. It could start a war, among other things," Sajan said, stepping a bit closer to Cassian.

"Ovidius will know better than to wage war with me. He will not like it, but he will not deny me either. Now, do as I say. Something tells me our time in this city is limited," Cassian ordered.

"Master, they've grounded all aircrafts," Chloe said.

Alexias and Alexis rolled their eyes and Aaron stifled the smirk and any remark he may have wanted to make that it would seem even the *Elite* could be "stupid" as he had been accused of being.

"You're point, Chloe?" Cassian turned toward her.

"Well, if we try to fly them to St. Louis, they'll shoot our plane down," she said.

"Really, Chloe?" Alexias gave her a sideways look. "We're not taking the jet."

"Oh." Chloe frowned. "This is going to be exhausting."

Cassian's expression grew hard. "It is my orders and it is necessary. Follow Alexis and Alexias; they will give you my instructions as I don't like repeating myself. I will contact you with more information soon. Right now, you have work to do." He dismissed his lieutenants with a wave of his hand.

The four vampires nodded and left the condo with their humans in tow.

Cassian turned towards Robert. "My cell phone, I need it."

Robert nodded and ran back into the master bedroom and returned as fast as he could, carrying the sleek, black iPhone. He handed it to Cassian.

"Gather a few of our belongings, only those we need. We don't have time to concern ourselves with luxuries," Cassian ordered.

"Yes, Master. Umm, may I ask who are you going to call?" Robert asked, the wavering in his tone betraying the brave face he tried to put on. Inside, he was terrified, his only comfort was in knowing that he was the Master's servant.

Cassian didn't answer him. Instead he punched several numbers on the touch screen then held the device up to his ear. Robert decided to leave it alone and left to carry out the order he'd been given. He pulled two of his designer duffel bags from the hall closet and walked into his Master's bedroom first to gather a few articles of clothing and other important items.

Cassian waited several seconds until finally, his call was answered. "I'm sure you're aware of my current crisis," he said, foregoing a polite greeting.

Ovidius groaned. "Aware and concerned. My territory isn't far from yours and those zombies are killing and reanimating at an astronomical rate."

"They are. Which is why I need to seek shelter for my vampires and myself in your territory—I wouldn't make this request unless I had no other option," he said the last line through gritted teeth hoping he didn't sound as annoyed as he felt. The last thing he ever wanted to do was need another vampire Master to offer him and his protection. Especially not one he had turned himself. A vampire indebted to another was never a good situation to be in. Albeit, it was an unavoidable necessity at times like now.

"That may cause a problem, surely you can appreciate my concerns," Ovidius said.

"It would still be your territory. I have no desire to claim it. However, if this virus spreads, more cities will be in my predicament. Maybe even yours. We should combine our forces now, strike preemptively before we're caught off guard. I've taught you that much, I know."

Ovidius sighed. If it was one thing he knew, it was his sire's ironclad will to survive made even more frightening by his merciless and methodical means to ensure his survival. If he were to deny Cassian entry into his territory, it would be a declaration of war—one he'd lose. He was no fool and his desire to survive was just as strong. He thought briefly about his answer.

"As long as you respect my territory, we can work together."

"Excellent. I will instruct my vampires to go to you. They will be accompanied by a few humans we're trying to save."

"Why bother to waste time saving random humans when I have plenty here?" Ovidius asked, curious about his sire's actions.

"These will not be random humans. Understand, Ovidius, I'm standing in my living room looking down at what could possibly be the end of humanity if this epidemic can't be stopped. At this point, every human life we save guarantees our own. This virus, whatever it is, can affect us as well."

"What?!" Ovidius' voice increased a few octaves in his bewilderment.

"You see, now, why I am so concerned? One of the vampires in my territory was attacked and he went into a bloodlust rage and I'm sure he isn't the only one. All he could remember is the hunger. If enough of us are infected, especially repeatedly, we can drastically deplete our food source. Vampires cannot allow that to happen. *I* cannot allow that to happen and neither should you."

"Is this vampire you speak of still infected?" Ovidius asked, the uncertainty he felt was evident in his tone.

"I really have no way of knowing. He appeared to be of sound mind when he came to me and his thirst for blood seemed to have waned," Cassian replied.

"This is going to get much worse before it gets better. Send me your people. I'll have mine prepare a few of my properties where we can protect our investment."

"Fucking humans," Cassian cursed, thinking about the current events. "We'll need locations with more resources than your current properties. The humans will need space, food, water... other amenities. We'll also need buildings where windows are limited and doors can be easily monitored and fortified."

There was a short pause while Ovidius pondered. "I have a few ideas."

"Enlighten me."

"But first, are you sure we're not overreacting at this point?"

"Ovidius, if you were standing where I am right now, you wouldn't be questioning me. Do you realize, if vampires can be infected, just how quickly this will spread?" Cassian's tone had grown darker as did his mood. "If these steps we're taking prove to be—"

"I simply prefer to wait before exposing ourselves to the humans. What you're talking about doing will no doubt cause hysteria among them. It has only been a few hours, give the humans time to find the problem and fix it," Ovidius suggested.

Cassian huffed. His hand wrapped tightly around his phone as he struggled not to throw it against the wall in a fit of rage—or crush it for that matter. Instead he took another deep breath before speaking.

"They have lost control of this city. Those things are faster and stronger than the humans and already this virus has spread to the outer cities and suburbs of Chicago. You're territory of St. Louis isn't that far away when you really think about it, especially when these creatures have no need to rest. The only thing that slows them down is when they're killing. The government will no doubt attempt to quarantine this area. Their only recourse is to lay bombs to this city, but it's already too late. However, it won't stop them from trying. Meanwhile, the virus will continue to spread and while you're sitting back worrying about exposing vampires to the world, we'll be losing the advantage to protect our food source." He paused to give his child a chance to mull over what he'd said. "St. Louis is your territory and part of my agreement with you is to allow you to run your territory as you see fit. If you chose to not heed my warning, I'll accept that. I simply hope we won't suffer a worse fate in the end."

"My God, Cassian, the world isn't coming to an end. There's still time to see where this is heading. Bring your people, if it looks like matters are completely out of control, we'll take action as you suggested. Fair enough?"

"I have to abandon my home right now. Those creatures are in my building, killing and turning the residents as we speak. From where I stand, the world is ending. However, we'll do it your way. I have to wrap up one thing here before I settle there. I will bring you my servant, though. Thank you for your hospitality."

"See you soon," Ovidius ended the call.

"Idiot," Cassian hissed as he slipped his phone into his pocket. He turned facing Robert. "Is that everything we need?"

Robert nodded. "Just the necessities as you requested. What is it you needed to do before we go to St. Louis?" As far as he was concerned, the further away from Chicago, the better.

"I want to check out this SciTech Labs since it's been reported as the point of origin."

"Do I have to go with you?" Robert asked nervously.

"Of course not. Your weakness will only hinder me. I'm taking you to St. Louis where you'll be safe... at least for the time being. Come." Cassian beckoned for his servant.

Aaron coughed disruptively, purposely bringing attention to himself.

"Yes?" Cassian inquired.

"Well, what about me, Master? What do you want me to do?" he asked humbly.

Cassian smirked. "I have a very important job for you."

Aaron eyes grew wider with excitement as he awaited his new orders.

"I want you to contact as many vampires as you can, organize them and prepare them to leave the city immediately. They are to head to St. Louis where they will follow the instructions and rules, mind you, of the current Master there, as we will be his guest for the time being. Do you understand?" Cassian studied the young vampire before him.

Aaron nodded. "Yes, Master, I understand." He turned, leaving the condo. He knew he had to be careful upon exiting the building. The last thing he wanted to do was be bitten again.

"Shall we go, Master?" Robert asked. He had stood silently as the two vampires spoke, as was expected of a human servant.

Cassian nodded. "We shall."

Robert approached him carrying two duffel bags full of clothes and cash and one cooler filled with the Master's rare blood supply. Cassian turned back toward the window and with one great blow, punched through the glass sending shards down to the streets. He walked back to his sword, snatching it up then he wrapped one arm around Robert's waist and hoisted him upward as he levitated. His powers were drastically weakened during the day and flying was going to take a lot of strength on his part. It was also going to take longer than it would have had he gone at night. But he had no choice. Cassian pointed himself in the direction of St. Louis and propelled himself forward.

***

Standing on the roof of the Trump Tower, the four lieutenants looked at one another, then at their human servants.

Sajan turned toward the twins. "All right, what is his master plan?" he asked, with arms folded across his chest.

"Cassian's master plan is relatively simple. We're to gather as many humans who can better serve us in the event that this virus gets completely out of control," Alexias said.

"Like if every city looked just like Chicago, 'out of control'?"

Patrick asked, presenting the question to anyone willing to answer.

"Exactly." Alexis stated. "Perhaps it would be best if we took our human servants to the new location."

"Ugh, I hate flying during the day. It's going to take so much longer with my power only at half mast," Chloe complained.

"It'll take much longer the more time you spend bitching about it," Sajan remarked.

Chloe refrained from releasing the scathing, yet witty, comeback she had at the tip of her tongue.

Being Second in Command, he outranked her and therefore, he could speak to her any way he chose. Still, it didn't settle well with her, especially not in front of her human servant. Sajan watched the silent battle rage within the feisty female vampire and he couldn't stop the smirk that appeared at the tip of his lips.

She knows her place, he thought to himself. "Before we leave the city, we need to take at least one other human with us. To best use our time effectively, we should split up. I'll search downtown. Alexis, you take the south side, Alexias—the north. Chloe—the west side. These will be our targets until we're given orders otherwise, understand?" Sajan watched the others waiting for confirmation.

"Understood," they said in unison.

"We will work with the lords in each of our territories so that we can save as many humans as we can as quickly as we can. For those too weak for flight, leave them to organize other low level vampires to vacate the city," Sajan added.

"Is that all?" Chloe asked.

"For now." He wrapped his arm around the waist of his human servant. "Let's go."

The other vampires followed his lead and took their humans into their arms before lifting off, flying toward their targeted areas to search.

***

After Aaron left Cassian's condo, he called his vampire friends, some answered some didn't. He hoped the ones who didn't were still asleep and not draining the city dry like he had. Jesse didn't answer and that worried Aaron. But first he told the ones who did answer what Cassian said. Some didn't want to believe him, but when he'd challenged them, none wanted to ignore the Master's command even if it might be a joke. He told them to spread the word to every vampire they knew and so on.

After that he started his decent down the stairway. Aaron used every vampire move he had to avoid getting caught by the zombies. Having had several encounters with them, he had learned a few of their weaknesses. He was still beaming that the Master had entrusted him with a very important job. One he would have given to his lieutenants had they not been given other orders. He wanted to impress Cassian and force the Master to acknowledge his worthiness.

He ran to Jesse's place, bypassing the zombies there. The front door to Jesse's apartment was untouched, unlike some of the doors he's passed along the way. He broke through the door himself, shattering the lock with a strong turn of the knob. Then he pushed as forcibly as he could without making a lot of noise until he knocked the bolt lock off the door. He closed the door behind him and placed a heavy cabinet in front of it as silently as he could. He knew some of the zombies were on still on the floor looking for victims. Quickly, he went to Jesse's bedroom and knocked on his reinforced steal door. Jesse opened the door after several attempts to rouse him. He looked at Aaron through sleepy eyes. They began to grow bigger as he took in his best friend's appearance.

"What the fuck happened to you?" Jesse asked, his face a total mask of confusion and curiosity.

"We need to get the fuck out of this city," was Aaron's direct reply. "There's zombies attacking the humans and us. We can get infected, too." He made sure to whisper.

"What?" Jesse was even more confused. "Why are you whispering?"

"Jesse, I'm not fucking around. I've been to see Cassian and he wanted me to gather as many of his vampires as I could and get the hell out of Chicago. I've been spreading the word as fast as I can. I need you to do the same. Call all of the vampires you know and have them leave. We're to go to St. Louis. The Master there is expecting us."

"You're really serious?"

"Fuck! Yes, I'm serious. Do you not see all this fucking blood on me?" Aaron gestured to his person. "We can get bit and turned into one of those things, too. It happened to me, twice. I just went on like two blood binges, there's no telling how many people I killed. Now listen, we have to go. Those things are already in your building. You'll see for yourself soon."

Jesse trusted his friend even though he didn't understand the situation. Without any further opposition, he went back into his bedroom and took a peek out of the window, that's when he saw it.

"Fuck me," he gasped.

"Told you," Aaron said from the door way.

"Shit, what the fuck is going on?"

"Don't know, really."

Jesse dressed quickly, taking his wallet and cell. Then he went into the kitchen removing his blood supply and placing it inside an insulated cooler bag.

"Okay, let's get the fuck out of here," he said.

"Let's take the window."

"Fine with me."

"And when we get out there, follow my lead. Trust me. You don't want to get bit by one of those things."

"Would I attack you if I am?"

"You probably would and I'd have to kill you."

"Duly noted."

"Okay, let's go."

Both men jumped from Jesse's sixth floor apartment and immediately took off running. He followed Aaron's lead, avoiding the zombies along the way as best he could.

Chapter Six

The helicopter hovered over Philip and Clare's suburban home. Clare had gathered every bit of information she could find and packed it away in two boxes. She waited in her attic with her two children for Vincent to arrive. She looked down at the zombies who were trying to climb the walls of her home to reach her. The noise of the helicopter had drawn them in to everyone's dismay. Their pounding on the steal window shutters dented the metal and it would only be a matter of time before the shutters gave in just like that rooftop door. And they all knew it.

"Vincent, hurry!" she screamed as she shielded her eyes from the wind and dust being kicked up by the helicopter's blades.

"We're sending a basket, put the kids into it with the research," Vincent yelled back.

The soldiers began to lower a basket large enough for two adults toward the attic window. As instructed, Clare placed each of her children into the basket quickly, then she added the two boxes containing her husband's, modem, research papers, laptop and whatever else she could find. Slowly, the basket began to ascend back into the helicopter. Below, the zombies continued to bash their bodies against the steel barriers, weakening the joints and frames.

"Oh my God, please help me! Help me!" Clare cried as she leaned out the window waving her hands at the helicopter. She looked down at the monsters trying to get inside her home. Many she recognized as her neighbors. There was James Bowmen, wearing nothing but a pair of blood-soaked jeans. He was among them, both of his arms had been ripped from his bloody half-eaten torso exposing far too much of his insides. He stared up at her while jumping repeatedly in her rose bushes as if he could propel himself toward her. His black eyes rabid with hunger. It sent chills down her spine unlike anything she'd ever felt.

"Please help me!" Clair cried out again. She didn't want what happened to James and her husband to happen to her.

"Clare, be careful, wait. We're coming for you now," Vincent yelled, hoping to keep her from panicking and falling.

The window shutters in the living room gave in and several zombies climbed their way inside the home. The basket began to lower again with a soldier inside.

"Hurry, they're coming!" Sarah and Felicia screamed as they saw the house filling with more zombies.

Clare became more frantic when she heard the zombies banging on the attic door. She screamed and climbed onto the window seal using her knees to balance. She reached out towards the soldier who was coming closer for her. He leaned over, hooking his arms around her torso. He could see the zombies break through the door with one thing in their sights.

"Pull me up!" the solider yelled as she encircled her arms around his neck.

One of the zombies wrapped its hand around Clare's ankle, pulling her back inside the window. She shrieked and tried to snatch her leg away. The basket tilted to the side from her weight as she clung to the soldier with everything she had. The soldier struggled to keep himself inside the basket and to bring her with him. She screamed in excruciating pain as teeth began to rip into her limb, devouring her. She held on tightly to the soldier as she struggled to get away, but the zombies gripped flesh and clothes, pulling her from the soldier's grip and back into the attic. Clare's children screamed and cried for their mother as they watched her being dragged back into the house. Samantha and William held both kids, shielding them from seeing their mother being eaten alive through the attic window.

Samantha cradled Jasmine's head against her bosom, as she whispered in her ear. "It's going to be okay, it's going to be okay..." It was the only comforting words she could think of at the time and she had no idea if they were helping the child or not. She tried her best to hide her own horror and fear in hopes of keeping the little girl from going into shock. William was doing something similar with the young boy, Thomas, who was struggling in his arms as he fought to get away. The child screamed for his mother as he twisted and turned in William's unfailing grip.

Back inside the attic, Clare's fingers gripped the edge of the window sill as she tried desperately to hold on as long as she could. Tears flowed from her eyes as her intestines were being ripped from her abdomen. Blood poured from her mouth as she begged for the soldier to save her. Seeing that he couldn't, the soldier pressed himself against the other side of the basket as he pulled out his gun, firing the entire clip at the zombies who were now climbing over Clare's body to get to him. Several bullets struck the zombies. Two were shot in the head. Their bodies fell out of the window landing on the rose garden below. The helicopter pilot began to pull away from the house just as two of the zombies leaped forward, grabbing hold of the basket. The soldier inside screamed as he fired the last two bullets at the zombie closest to him. One of the bullets struck the zombie in the head and he fell down to the streets. The other zombie continued to climb up the basket, rounding the edge.

Sergeant Hicks fired his weapon at the zombie trying to attack his fellow soldier, but the swinging of the basket made it difficult to get a head shot. He was also trying to avoid shooting the soldier as well.

"Keep this bird steady!" Sgt. Hicks ordered.

The solider fighting for his life smashed the butt of his gun against the zombie's fingers and head, but the monster, dressed in a jogging outfit, kept moving forward. He pressed himself against the back of the basket in a last ditch effort to defend himself. He kicked at the zombie's head as it climbed up, its black eyes staring forward at its prey. Blood and bits of flesh clung to its lips and teeth as he moved forward with only one thought in mind—*feed*. The soldier struggled with the zombie, pitting all of his strength against his attacker. The zombie inched closer, its teeth snapping at the soldier's neck.

"Shit, do something!" Vincent screamed.

The helicopter pilot, remembering what happened to his partner earlier, took matters into his own hands.

"Hold on!" he yelled at the others. He steered the helicopter sharply, tilting it as he slammed the basket into a brick house. The basket listed to the side and the chain snapped. Both the soldier and the zombie fell three stories down, their bodies slamming onto the concrete. Vincent and the others watched horror-stricken as the zombies converged on the human, ripping his clothes and flesh with their teeth and nails. The solider screamed even as Hicks continued to fire his weapon. Finally, one of his bullets struck the soldier between the eyes, silencing him and sparing him a grizzly resurrection, he hoped. The zombies surrounding the soldier's corpse ripped the body apart, tearing limbs away as they feasted.

"What have we done?" Vincent whispered in disbelief.

Hicks growled in anger, pain and frustration. He looked at the pilot and made an attempt to rush towards him, but William and Dr. Powers held the soldier at bay.

"You need to calm down," Dr. Powers urged.

"What the fuck was that? You just don't abandon a soldier!" Sgt. Hicks yelled.

"I did what I had to do to protect the rest of us on this helicopter. I'm sorry," the pilot said.

"Look, I know you're in pain and in shock, but we need to keep a steady head," William told Hicks. "You aren't the only one suffering." with his eyes, he gestured to the two children who had just lost their last remaining parent.

Hicks huffed and puffed for a few seconds as he forced himself to calm down. "Let me go," he ordered the two men holding him.

"Are you all right? We can't have you attacking the pilot out of revenge," Dr. Powers said.

"I know my mission," Hicks said. "Now get your fucking hands off me."

Dr. Powers and William exchanged looks, but both men released their hold on Hicks and took a step back. William returned to his seat and put his arm around the boy pulling the wailing child in closer.

"Are we sure this is everything?" Sarah asked, holding one of the two boxes. Her hands shook uncontrollably with fear and she felt a millions butterflies fluttering around in her stomach making her want to vomit. Her eyes were clouded with tears and she tried hard to regain her composure.

"It's going to have to be enough. We can't risk going back in there to find out and we need what fuel we have left to get to Springfield," Felicia said.

Sarah thought about what the scientist said and nodded. She looked over at the two crying and frightened children being held by William and Samantha. She wanted to comfort them. They had just witnessed their mother being eaten alive and their father was one of the first casualties.

Who else did they have left in this world to take care of them and would those people even still be alive? She wondered. Then she looked at Vincent, he sat silently on the floor of the helicopter where he had been leaning out to talk to Clare. He stared forward as if in shock. Quickly, she went over to him, taking his face into her hands.

"Vincent, honey, are you okay?" Sarah yelled over the roaring sound of the rotating blades and motor. She lightly brushed a few dark strands of hair from his eyes as she monitored him.

"What have I done?" Vincent asked himself again.

Hicks grunted. "I don't have the patience for this shit. Get it together. We don't have time for your pity party."

"I agree. We need you to snap out of it, Doctor Masterson. We won't be able to retrieve the data from SciTech Labs without you. We're going to need you to talk whatever retrieval team we assemble through it all and then we need to pray they make it out alive," Dr. Powers said.

"I know! I just saw my friend's wife get ripped apart. I'm trying to think!" Vincent said in his defense.

"Vincent, honey..." Sarah said, gaining his attention. When he looked up at her, she nodded toward the two children.

Vincent nodded.

"A lot more people are going to die if we don't start being more productive," Dr. Powers pointed out.

"I know," Vincent said. He rubbed the tears from his eyes and shook himself. He looked at Sarah. "I'll be okay, baby." He leaned forward, kissing her lips, then her forehead.

Sarah gave him a smile that didn't quite reach her eyes. She was still worried about him and no amount of words could make her worry less. She settled down beside him as he wrapped his arm around her shoulder.

"So it's actually confirmed that a team has been assembled?" Felicia inquired.

"Just received the word," Dr. Powers said.

"So I'll be directing the retrieval team?" Vincent asked.

"Yes."

"I'm glad we're doing it this way, we can't afford to have you risk your life," Felicia said.

Hicks grimaced and snorted. "What? The life of a soldier holds no value?"

Felicia turned to Hicks. "Excuse me?"

Hicks leaned forward. "Un-freaking-believable."

"Sgt. Hicks, this kind of conversation will not yield results. So, let's not go there, shall we?" Dr. Powers stated.

"No. If Sgt. Hicks has a problem with something I said, I'm more than willing to clarify myself," Felicia said. "Sgt. Hicks, would you consider it wise to send Dr. Masterson into a possibly dangerous environment where he probably will not make it out alive knowing full well he's a person of interest who may have an idea about what needs to be done to save the human race?" She looked at him with one eyebrow cocked, awaiting his response.

Hicks' jaw tightened as he ground his teeth together. As much as he hated to admit it to himself or anyone, she was right. He turned, looking out of the window.

"I take your silence as evidence that you would agree with me after all," Felicia stated.

"In the fact that he is necessary, but not that his life is more valuable. That soldier we just lost, Private Jones, he had a wife and kids, too. Those men under my command who were slaughtered on that helicopter, they had families as well. They aren't just acceptable losses, not to me. We do what we do because someone has to and it's important. I don't like anyone thinking we're expendable, do you understand me?" Sgt. Hicks looked at Felicia.

She nodded. "Fair enough."

"As long as we understand each other," Hicks said.

"We do," Felicia replied.

"Did any one notice back there that those zombies didn't get up after being shot in the head?" Hicks pointed out.

"Yes, they did," Vincent said.

"But not right away." Hicks looked at the others. "There was at least a thirty second pause between those zombies taking one to the brain and them getting back up again."

"In all of the confusion, I didn't notice that," Vincent said.

"I did," Felicia stated. "But when they didn't stay down, I knew a bullet to the head wouldn't kill them."

"But it's a start," Dr. Powers said, holding one finger up thoughtfully. "Eventually, we're going to need to capture one of those things and study it. That's been our plan since the first outbreak was reported, we just haven't had any success."

"This shit is depressing," Sarah mumbled to herself.

"We need to gather every lead scientist in the country and put them on this," Samantha said.

"We're already ahead of you. Several are flying in to collaborate on what we should do," Dr. Powers informed.

"Please tell me that location isn't anywhere near Chicago," William commented.

"It's the CDC in Atlanta," Dr. Powers said.

"Why didn't you just say that?" William snorted, then shook his head as if to say "idiot".

"I have my own way of doing things," Dr. Powers said with a shrug.

"How long until we get there?" Samantha asked.

"First, we'll land in Springfield, IL. We need to send the team into SciTech Labs as soon as possible. We have the communication center set up at the IDPH building there. Once we get what we need, we'll be taking a plane to Atlanta," Dr. Powers said.

Samantha sighed. "I meant Springfield. How long till we get there?"

Dr. Powers looked at his watch and then conferred with the pilot before responding. "Looks like we'll be there in about twenty-five... maybe thirty minutes."

"Any more updates about the current situation?" Felicia inquired.

"I'm getting a steady feed of information," Dr. Powers said, pressing the headset closer to his ear. "We were already aware that the outbreak extended to the south side as well as the far west and north sides of Chicago and in some suburbs by the time we got to you."

"I think the city-wide police evacuations expedited the spread of the disease," Felicia said. "Think about it, more people fleeing their homes and the city are finding themselves trapped in traffic. They're sitting ducks when those zombies come running down the streets. That's how more of those things are being made. It's no wonder this disease or virus, or whatever it is, is spreading so fast."

"Does the president know how bad it's gotten here?" Sarah asked, looking around the helicopter.

Dr. Powers nodded. "He's been made aware and relocated to a safe location."

"Shit, can we go where *he's* at?" Sarah remarked.

"What's he doing to prevent this from spreading outside state lines?" Vincent asked. A part of him didn't want to know the answer. If the movies were telling the truth, then Chicago and its citizens both dead and alive could count on being barbequed very soon.

"That's the bad news. This epidemic has already passed state lines. I'm receiving reports of outbreak in Michigan, Wisconsin, Indiana... hell, even Iowa and I have no idea how the hell it spread that damn far," Dr. Powers informed them.

Vincent's eyebrows shot up. "What the fuck? These things are on foot right? I've seen them move, they're fast, but they aren't so damn fast that they can cover that many miles in so little time," he said.

"We have no idea. The reports I've been getting resemble what we're seeing here in Chicago and nothing we currently know of can explain that jump in distance from Ground Zero," Sgt. Hicks said.

Dr. Powers frowned, a grim expression distorting his usually handsome features. "With an outbreak of this magnitude, there's really only one thing that can be done to contain it or at least slow it down. It's not pretty and it'll cost millions, if not billions in the long run, but what choice do we have?"

"Are they going to firebomb this city?" Sarah asked, looking from Dr. Powers to Sgt. Hicks.

Hicks' lips tightened into a straight line. "I'm not privy to the President's orders, but I'm sure we'll find out soon. Of course, the smart thing would be to quarantine the city, or at this point, the state."

"Nuke the city, you mean, or the state?" Sarah insinuated.

"I'm not at liberty to say," Hicks stated.

Sarah was silent for a few moments as she reflected on everything that would be lost—everything and everyone. She took a deep, shuddering breath. As sad as the thought was, doing so would hopefully save lives. She held Vincent's hand in her own, her thumb gently rubbing his fingers.

"Well, in any case, I think it would be best if we got as far away from the state as possible, like Japan," she said.

Dr. Powers nodded. "That's still the plan, well, not Japan... at least not right now."

"Did the FAA ground all flights?" Felicia asked.

"The FAA was ordered to ground all aircraft unless otherwise authorized immediately after getting word from the CDC. As far as I know, the planes that landed in other states haven't reported any outbreaks."

"At least not yet," Vincent murmured.

"What was that, Doctor?" Dr. Powers asked, his eyes scanning Vincent's as if looking for more information he feared the doctor was holding back.

"Just the time discrepancy we talked about earlier," Vincent reminded.

Felicia nodded grimly. "There is that."

"I'm hoping a bitten person can be saved," Felicia speculated.

"That's the answer we're all working towards," Dr. Powers stated as he leaned over, looking out of the window. "Jesus Christ, would you look at this."

The others followed him, looking out of several windows at the colossal traffic jam stalling the interstate. Cars were bumper to bumper as frustrated and terrified drivers beeped and yelled at each other. Hundreds of drivers had decided to abandon their automobiles, opting to flee on foot taking only what they could carry. Vincent frowned, knowing that they would soon fall victim to those monsters. With nowhere to hide and no way of running, their fates were already doomed. It was just a matter of time now.

"Those people down there, they're going to die, aren't they?" Sarah asked as tears streamed down her cheeks again.

Vincent didn't want to tell her what he was thinking. It was just too damn dispiriting. He didn't answer her—no one did. He looked at the two children being held and comforted by William and Samantha. They were still crying for the loss of their mother. He had no way of knowing if they were aware that their father was dead as well.

My God, what have we done? Vincent thought to himself once again.

"What's the current situation on the retrieval team?" He decided he was going to focus all of his thoughts and energy on coming up with a cure. It was the one hopeful thing he could cling to.

"They should be arriving in Chicago by the time we get to Springfield give or take a few minutes. It's a small team and I don't know if that's a good thing or bad. Unfortunately, most of our resources were sent out to get a handle on the situation. As we all know, that didn't work out so well and we're down a lot of men. They know it's a priority, based on what you've said, so we'll get more information on that when we get to Springfield," Dr. Powers said as he typed furiously on his tablet.

Vincent leaned forward a bit to try and sneak a peek, but was unsuccessful. Giving up, he decided to sit down in one of the available seats. The movement of the helicopter as it made a slight turn caused his stomach to make threats of releasing bile. He swallowed hard as he fought down his nausea.

"Here, let me help you up." Vincent took Sarah's hand into his own, squeezing it gently as he helped her rise.

"Thanks," she said, taking the seat next to his.

"I'm so sorry," he whispered into her ear.

"I know." Sarah leaned her forehead against his as she cuddled closer to him. "We'll pull through this, baby. God help us all."

***

Cassian landed softly on the front patio of Ovidius' home. He released his human servant, Robert, who tried his best to finger-comb his wind-whipped, dark hair. The front door opened without him needing to knock and Roman, Ovidius' human servant stood before them.

"My Master is expecting you," Roman announced with a bow.

"Take me to him," Cassian ordered.

Roman nodded and turned, leading them to where his Master was waiting. Ovidius was sitting on his plush leather sofa watching the news on his gigantic seventy-two inch, LCD television screen.

"Your vampires have yet to arrive," Ovidius said by way of greeting.

"As you know, most are too young and must travel by other means of transportation. My more powerful vampires are on their way," Cassian remarked. "Although, I could do without your attitude. I don't want to be in this predicament any more than you do."

"I can't argue with that. What about your lieutenants and lords? I assume they'll be dropping off their humans?

Cassian nodded curtly. "Eventually, they will. I gave them orders prior to coming here." He turned his gaze towards the humongous television set. "Enjoying the chaos?"

Ovidius snorted. "Glib as ever."

"Incredulous, would be a more fitting description of my current mood," Cassian corrected. "Well, are you?"

"I find this to be amazing," Ovidius said, casually, as he gestured toward the television.

"I find it to be more of a disappointment and inconvenience, if anything." Cassian observed his friend's relaxed demeanor and frowned. "I'm thrilled that you're taking this as lightly as you are."

Ovidius smirked. "I have yet to meet anyone who makes sarcasm sound so menacing and patronizing at the same time quite like you, Cassian." He turned around, facing his sire. "For your information, I'm not taking this lightly. I'm monitoring the situation closely."

"Ah, yes. From your presumably safe position on the sofa, I see. If you were out there on the streets, you'd already be acting on my recommendations," Cassian commented as he surveyed the room's interior. "Such common taste in decorating. Really, Ovidius, have I taught you nothing of class?"

Ovidius sighed. "For both of our sakes, I hope the humans can get this situation under control as soon as possible."

Cassian remained silent. Holding his tongue wasn't something he did often—or at all for that matter. He didn't answer to anyone, nor was he used to having to make compromises. One thing he could agree on, he did want the situation to be resolved.

Ovidius looked his sire up from head to toe and his gaze settled on the sword in his sire's hand. "I hope you're just trying to save a memento from your youth."

Cassian glanced at his sword then back at Ovidius. "Do not worry, it's not for you."

"I thought not. I've had my servant prepare your rooms—"

"Have you heard of the attacks in Iowa?" Cassian interjected.

Ovidius' lips tightened as he kept his anger in check. "As I've said, I'm aware of the situation as it progresses."

"Then you have an idea of how fast these things are traveling. They've already breached the state lines. St. Louis isn't that far away."

"Let's not beat around the bush, Cassian. Bottom line is I'm not willing to expose vampires to the humans until it's absolutely necessary."

"What if by then, it's too late?" Cassian pointed out. "And who's to say they aren't already aware that we exist?"

"I'm sure I would have heard something on the news if they knew about us at this point," Ovidius said.

"Maybe not. There were no cameras capturing a young vampire in my territory attack on a rescue helicopter. But I'm sure someone somewhere may have witnessed it."

"As if they would have any inkling of what they thought they saw. With those things running wild, they probably assumed he was one of them," Ovidius speculated.

"You're far too old to be this naïve." Cassian sighed. "With an epidemic like this, we cannot hide in the darkness for much longer."

"What would you have me do, Cassian?" Ovidius' eyes studied his sire carefully.

"I would have you take action. If we are exposed, so be it. It's a risk we must take if we are to survive," Cassian said as he made his way closer to the sofa and Ovidius.

"As I recall, this was a fear vampires had during the reign of the Bubonic Plague. The "Black Death," they called it."

Cassian frowned thoughtfully. "This is no mere virus such as the plague, or any that came before or preceded it up to this point. We have never been affected and humans, though less savory, were still our prey. As far as I'm concerned, these things may not even be a food source. If their bite can turn us rabid, then their blood is probably just as dangerous. So you see, this depletes our food source at an exponential rate and it renders us ferocious without rhyme or reason except for the insatiable need to kill and feed. There may be other effects we still don't know about. We cannot afford to have our kind succumb to such an affliction…"

Cassian leaned forward, placing a hand on his protégé's shoulder as he locked his blue eyes to Ovidius' green. "Ovidius, a great leader knows when he must risk all to save his people. I have already taken steps to ensure that we have a chance and I am sure I do not stand alone in my preparation. Join me to save our kind, this is all that matters. Please do not take my suggestions as subterfuge or a challenge. My only interest is in the survival of our race. Not your territory or power over the vampires who reside here."

Ovidius licked his lips, moistening them as he pondered Cassian's words. He was never one to ignore the obvious or to turn his back on sound advice. After a few seconds, he nodded.

"You have always guided me well, Cassian. If you believe it is necessary to expose ourselves at this junction, then I will stand beside you. What are your thoughts?"

Cassian nodded quickly, satisfied that his words had finally penetrated. "We must seek out locations that have a vast number of resources. The humans we save will need food, water, clothing and other necessities. To maintain order, we must make sure that we are in control of all resources."

Ovidius sat back, running a finger along the smooth flesh of his bottom lip. "Costco comes to mind. It is well stocked with an assortment of items and it has limited windows and access points. Not to mention it's own gas station."

Cassian nodded slowly as he mentally scanned his memory of the location.

"What about a shopping mall?" Robert suggested.

Both vampires turned toward him, which made him a bit nervous. He knew that he had spoken out of turn, but something had compelled him to speak out. He switched from one foot to the other as his fingers fidgeted with the straps of the duffel bags he was still holding.

"Come again?" Cassian arched an eyebrow as he waited for

him to elaborate.

Robert's palms began to sweat, but he took several breaths, calming himself down since his faux pas was being overlooked. No doubt in favor of the current emergency situation.

"Well, I guess, since vampires are going to make themselves known, might as well take over the huge location with even more resources. I mean, at least in a huge shopping mall, you have a ton of stores with clothes, food, tools, whatever they need or want. Plus there are places people can sleep and a food court where they can eat—places where food can be cooked."

Ovidius snorted. "Had your human kept his tongue as he is supposed to, he would have learned that his suggestion was already a part of my plan."

"Is that so?" Cassian cocked an eyebrow. "My human forgot his place, but I applaud him for trying... to a point. Unfortunately, with a shopping mall, there are many windows and entry points. It will need serious reinforcing with materials even vampires will have difficulty breaking through. … Truth be told, I don't think we have the time. With your delaying the necessary actions that needed to be taken, our options have also dwindled."

"The location I mentioned will have to suffice, then. It's most certainly large enough," Ovidius stated with a hint of agitation in his tone. He could tolerate his sire just fine when he was in Chicago and there was a nice distance between them. But this co-existence was going to be a challenge for the both of them. He was no longer Cassian's protégé. He was his equal by Vampire law. A Master in his own right and he had complete reign of St. Louis.

Robert stood silent, still holding the heavy luggage, as the two vampires spoke. He didn't need to be a vampire to feel the intense heat between the two Masters. The air was thick with it and any wrong step could send this already tense situation spiraling. His bladder begged for release and his stomach was still queasy from the flight over. He really just wanted to lay down somewhere—after relieving himself, of course. However, he wasn't going to interrupt two Master vampires a second time, not on his life.

"What about a condo complex, like where you lived? It has plenty of living quarters and we can stock the bottom floors with resources to disperse among the humans?" Ovidius asked.

Cassian shook his head. "It leaves us far too vulnerable."

"Can these things climb buildings?"

"I am not fully aware of what they can or cannot do. However, I do know that vampires who are infected will be able to climb and fly. We cannot risk an infected vampire breaking into our stronghold and attacking our livestock of humans in a location where it would be difficult to maintain watch."

Ovidius nodded, understanding Cassian's reasoning. "Very well, I'll send my vampires out to secure the local Costco. I'll also send out others to find all of the extra materials will need to fortify this location."

"We won't be able to help everyone, but we can save enough to save ourselves and preserve the future of humanity," Cassian said. "This location will be its own resource."

Ovidius nodded.

"May I ask a question?" Robert looked at his Master, awaiting permission.

Cassian turned towards his human. "What is it, Robert?"

"Master, how are you going to take over those places during the day when vampires are at their weakest? With everything that's going on, humans will be on high alert and any actions you take might be treated with extreme prejudice. They—the humans I mean—might try to take the vampires out, even at the risk of the humans inside. I don't want anything to happen to them or to you," Robert said.

Cassian nodded slowly, his lips pursed as he carefully considered his human's concerns. "You prove a good point, Robert, one even I had overlooked." He smiled. "I knew there was a reason I chose you to serve me."

Robert grinned, pleased that his Master approved of him. "Thank you, Master. But really, you're so powerful, even now, when the sun is high in the sky. It was easy for you to overlook less powerful beings—"

Cassian held his hand up, silencing Robert. "I'm going to stop you right there. Your placating is taking you only so far before your words become insulting."

Robert bowed. "My apologies, Master. I didn't mean to insult."

"I know." Cassian shook his head as he wiped his brow.

Ovidius chuckled, in spite of the tense situation surrounding them. "His point is valid. People are no doubt raiding those locations now, looking for resources before fleeing the city. It won't be easy to take over those areas secretly. No doubt the authorities will be called into action. But I trust my lieutenants and lords to be able to handle it as smoothly as they can."

Cassian huffed. "We will have to do whatever is necessary. If this place is open, we close and barricade it trapping inside all the humans who happen to be there. If this location is closed, we take it over and began to transport humans there for safe keeping. I believe that the time will come when we won't have to fight to keep them in. They'll be begging us to protect them from what's coming."

"I'll get right on it. In the meantime, what will you be doing?" Ovidius inquired.

"I have to return to Chicago. There's a laboratory there where it's been reported as the point of the outbreak. I want to go there and see for myself if anything can be salvaged—people or research." Cassian turned to head for the door.

"Wait!" Ovidius called out.

Cassian stopped, turning towards him. "What is it?"

"Like I've said, I've been watching the news. Those grotesque things seem pretty invulnerable. Although, when they get shot in the head—that seems to slow them down," Ovidius warned.

"So, what are you saying?" Cassian arched an eyebrow.

"I wouldn't suggest taking these things head on. If you're going into the belly of the beast, as they say, take a weapon that will work better than a gun."

"Why do you think I have this?" Cassian raised the sword.

Ovidius smiled, revealing his pearly whites. "The warrior in me almost envies you."

"I'm sure you'll get your chance to spill blood."

"I was so good at it, remember?"

Cassian smiled in memory. "As if I could ever forget."

"Do you need assistance?"

"I have no idea what I'll be facing and in the unfortunate event that I am infected, I don't want to be in a position to easily infect others. Nor do I want to deal with an infected vampire when I'm trying to fend for myself and search for information."

"You could have easily just said, 'no'," Ovidius teased.

"I could have, but then you would have been wondering why not," Cassian winked.

"Very well then, do us a favor and don't get bitten. If what you told me is true, a vampire of your age and power would do a lot of damage if you're infected," Ovidius said. There was a slight frown on his face as he pondered the dreadful prospect.

Cassian placed a hand on his shoulder, squeezing gently in a reassuring gesture. "Don't worry, my friend. I don't intend on becoming one of those things, not even for a little while. Please take care of my people. I'm trusting you with them."

Ovidius placed his hand over Cassian's where it rested on his shoulder. "I'll take care of them as well as I take care of my own."

Satisfied with that answer, Cassian nodded and walked out of the room.

Ovidius looked at Robert. "Roman," he called.

His human servant entered the room. "Yes, Master?"

"This is Robert, Cassian's servant. Please show him to the room where they will be staying," Ovidius ordered. "For the moment, at least," he added as an afterthought.

Roman bowed and then gestured for Robert to follow him as he led him out of the room. Ovidius returned to his position on the sofa as he pulled his cell phone from his pocket, dialing the number to one of his lieutenants.

"Yes, Master?" Ericka answered, knowing who was calling by the number.

"Where is Logan?" Ovidius inquired.

"Master, he is still sleeping."

"Did I not tell you to wake him?"

"Master, I tried, but he has redesigned his morning sleeping chamber. It's locked from the inside and only he can open it. It's also soundproof," Ericka explained.

"How inconvenient," Ovidius growled. If he wasn't already encumbered by his sire's demands, oh wait... *suggestions,* having to physically wake his child up was more than a little annoying as far as he was concerned.

"I'll be there shortly." Ovidius ended the call, slipping his cell back into his pocket. He rose from the sofa just as Cassandra entered the den.

"So I heard Cassian, is he still here?" she asked, looking around the room.

"If you don't feel his presence, then he's not here," Ovidius snapped.

She turned sharply, her gaze settling on him. "Well, you're in a mood. I wasn't sure, you know. Cassian can shield his aura."

"I assure you, he didn't when he set foot into my home. But you're correct, I am in a mood. Apparently, Logan's installed a new sleeping chamber which is impenetrable to his human servant."

"Or any human and probably vampire dumb enough to try to enter during the day," Cassandra added.

"I'll praise him later for his ingenuity, but for now, I'll chastise him for putting me in this troublesome position." Ovidius walked toward the exit, stopping in the doorway. "In my stead, I want you to gather my vampires and have them secure the Costco and Target Pharmacy."

"The ones on Rusty road?" Cassandra asked both eyebrows raised in surprise. "I thought you were going to hold off on that?"

Ovidius nodded. "Initially, I was. However, Cassian is a hard man to shut out or shut down... especially when he's right."

"But we'll be exposing ourselves. What if it never reaches us?" Cassandra asked, clearly worried about the consequence.

"It was my concern, too. But I can't ignore the possibility that St. Louis will be in the same crisis that Chicago and other cities are currently in. At the rate this epidemic is spreading, that may be sooner rather than never. If there was ever a time to throw caution to the wind, it is now. I'd much rather be exposed, than caught off guard. Now, go and do as I say." With that, Ovidius walked out of the room, leaving the mansion entirely and heading towards Logan's home.

Chapter Seven

Ovidius landed softly on the front porch of Logan's two-story mansion. He pressed the ornate doorbell and waited with foot tapping for the vampire's servant to answer.

The door opened and a lovely vixen stood in the frame. Ericka's long black hair fell softly over one shoulder as her electric blue eyes peered at her Master. She bowed her head. "Master, please come in." She opened the door wider, stepping aside.

Ovidius entered, taking a quick look around. "Where's this new room Logan has constructed?"

"In the basement, Master. I can show you—"

Ovidius held up a hand, silencing her. "That won't be necessary; I can sense him on my own." He placed a hand on her arm. "I need you to gather all of the blood Logan has in storage. Pack it safely. Also, gather all of his swords... we'll need them."

Ericka didn't hesitate to carry out his orders. She nodded and turned, heading towards the kitchen to pack up the blood. Ovidius made his way into the basement, walking down the marble staircase. He followed the path down the long hallway, rounding the corner past several other rooms until he reached what could only be Logan's new sleeping chamber. A titanium door replaced the old oak one. There was a key pad, equipped with a retina and hand-print scanner. No doubt, it was the best in modern technology.

Ovidius pressed his hand against the titanium door and closed his eyes.

"Logan," he whispered as he concentrated his mental energy on his target. "Rise and come to me."

Very soon, he heard the locks disengage and the door opened with Logan standing on the other side naked and a bit disheveled.

"Master, to what do I owe the pleasure?"

"Get dressed. We have an emergency," Ovidius said.

"What kind of emergency?" Logan asked as he ran his fingers through his dark brown, unkempt locks.

"If I didn't see it with my own eyes, I would swear it was an elaborate hoax. Unfortunately, it's not. Chicago is being attacked by what the media is calling zombies and they'll be here soon. We need to prepare."

Logan stared at Ovidius for several seconds. "Are you serious?"

"When have you ever known me to tell a joke?" Ovidius cocked an eyebrow as he stared sternly at his child.

"You've told plenty."

"Today, I'm feeling rather serious and a bit peeved. Don't test me."

"I'll get dressed." Logan decided not to argue any longer.

"That'd be best. Meet me upstairs when you're done." Ovidius turned, heading back towards the staircase.

"Master, I've packed all of the spare blood that's in the house," Ericka announced upon Ovidius' return.

"Good. Are you aware of what's going on?" he asked.

She nodded. "For the past hour, I've been aware."

"And you did not think to contact me?"

Ericka gasped. Her heart-rate began to quicken as her brain registered the anger in Ovidius' tone. She lowered herself to one knee.

"Master, please forgive me. I had only wanted to protect Logan."

"As if you could from a threat of this magnitude. He was safest where he was at. You were the one who was in danger. It's my job to protect all of the vampires and their servants in my territory. The next time you are aware of a threat, you are obligated to contact me, is that clear?"

Ericka nodded. "Yes, Master. Crystal."

"She was only doing as I instructed, Ovidius," Logan said as he entered the room.

"You should train your human in the ways of vampire

etiquette."

"She knows. She knows she belongs to me. She knows her life is mine for the taking," Logan commented.

Ovidius smirked. "She should know that all must answer to me."

Logan gave him a slight nod. "She does... in all respects." He walked over to Ericka, brushing the back of his fingers along the delicate flesh of her jawline.

"My lovely," he whispered.

Ericka blushed and smiled. "My love," she replied.

"We have work to do," Ovidius stated. He didn't bother with tact as he let his annoyance show in his tone and body language. He stood there, arms crossed over his chest as he glared at them.

"Very well," Logan said, with a sigh. "What is our first order of business?"

"I want you to help Cassian. He's claimed he doesn't want help and doesn't need it... I fear that he will."

"And what if I incur his wrath when I arrive? I do not wish to be on the receiving end of his anger," Logan said.

"You are acting under my orders. He will not hold you responsible. However, I don't believe anger is what you'll be greeted with. I'll take your human with me for safe keeping. You, on the other hand will need to arm yourself with a sword."

Both of Logan's eyebrows shot up. "A sword?"

"Yes. These things are very difficult to kill. Bullets have very little effect on them and—I simply can't stress this enough—you cannot allow yourself to be bitten. Vampires are susceptible to this virus from what I've been told."

"A virus that can affect us? How is this so?!" Logan's eyebrows creased as he pondered this unsettling news.

"I do not know. That is what Cassian is trying to discover. You have your orders, go now," Ovidius commanded.

Logan nodded. He walked over to the pile of swords lying on his sofa that Ericka had gathered. He picked up one that he favored and left the mansion.

"You and I are leaving now." Ovidius approached the sofa and scooped up the swords.

Ericka gathered the cooler containing the blood then opened the door for him. Together they left the mansion and climbed into Logan's Cadillac Escalade.

"Where are we going to go, Master?" Ericka asked.

"I have my vampires securing two locations that will stand as our strongholds until this calamity is over."

"What if the police or army try to attack us?"

"We'll be prepared for that as well. My concern isn't the police; it's the things that are coming this way."

"Are we heading there now... to the stronghold, I mean?"

"Yes. That's where I'm taking you." Ovidius stopped the car abruptly when he hit gridlock traffic. Cars were bumper to bumper. Angry and panicked drivers honked horns and screamed at each other. He had flown to Logan's home and managed to avoid the growing traffic, but now it was worse than it was before.

"This isn't going to work," Ovidius said, looking around.

"What do we do now?" Ericka asked.

"I will have to secure the weapons as best I can. You will have to carry the cooler and I'll fly us there." Ovidius put the SUV in park and climbed out. He walked towards the back, opening the hatch door. After a quick search, he found a pair of jumper cables. He quickly tied them around the swords, holding them together.

"Ericka, let's go."

Ericka exited the SUV and walked away from the traffic and prying eyes into the trees. Ovidius slipped his arm around her waist. "Hold on to that container."

"I will, Master."

"Good." Ovidius took flight in the direction of Costco.

***

Ovidius landed on the rooftop of the huge shopping complex. He released Ericka, making sure she was steady on her feet. One of his vampires approached him, bowing her head, slightly.

"Master, we have taken over this location. Cassandra is waiting below," Madison informed.

"Did she have Roman and Robert with her?"

"Yes."

"Very good, and thank *you*. You've done well," Ovidius complemented—to Madison's utter delight.

She led both Ovidius and Ericka through the roof entrance that was currently being fortified by two vampires with a thick steel door. They traveled down the back stairs and into the main shopping area. Ovidius looked around. Some of the store's shelves were in disarray. Hundreds of items were scattered over the floor in various aisles. The scent of blood was fresh in the air, especially where several glass bottles had been broken. Three of the windows had been shattered, leaving the floor cluttered with dangerous shards.

Ovidius pointed to the exposed windows. "We need to secure those."

"We're on it, Master," Madison assured him. "This location has outside shutters and we'll be adding more protection from inside. Jared and Michael are going to use solid steel to cover all of the windows."

Ovidius nodded.

"Very good." He looked around. "And the people who were here?"

"Took us a minute to get them all under control. There are a little over two hundred people here. We have them confined to the back of the store over there." She pointed toward the far corner.

"Excellent. Are any infected?" Ovidius asked.

Madison shook her head. "Not that we could tell. Their blood smells fresh and it's pumping accurately. They're terrified. They think we're here to rob them or something. Jared did explain that we're here to protect them. Whether or not they believe him is another story."

He nodded. "Cell phones, laptops and tablets?"

"We had everyone remove them from their person the moment we took over. We took purses, backpacks, duffel bags, everything.

The telephone lines were shut down in preparation before we entered."

"Good. Now about the perimeter?" Ovidius gestured to the parking lot.

"I realize these things are strong and fast. They could easily climb a gate or fence. So I decided to surround the grounds with cargo trailers. I've got the vampires in my sector gathering tractor trucks with big enough trailers where we can line them up and even stack them up around the building leaving only one entrance to secure maximum protection and give us an overall peripheral advantage."

"Were you able to take over this location without showing supernatural abilities?"

Madison smiled then nodded. "We were." She reached behind and pulled the 45mm handgun from her pants, showing it off. "They think we're humans holding them hostage for some ransom. We've already had several pleas of 'we'll give you whatever you ask,' blah, blah." She rolled her eyes.

Ovidius chuckled. "Excellent. This is why you're one of my most prized vampires. You're ability to make the most rational decisions."

Madison winked. "This is why I am your *best* lieutenant."

He laughed. "Ah, I would think Logan and Cassie would strongly disagree."

"Let them. The truth can't be argued." She bit her bottom lip as she fought to contain her inner glee that her actions had pleased her Master. She didn't want the squeal of joy to leak out and make her look immature in his eyes.

Ovidius caressed the back of her neck, pulling her head forward as he planted a soft kiss on her forehead.

"I am pleased," he said before letting her go.

"I wish to address our captives." He followed Madison as she led him to where they were keeping the humans. The people were huddled together. Some were standing, others sitting, but all were in one section. The look of panic and uncertainty was evident on their faces as their eyes settled on the newest player entering the room.

"Ladies and gentlemen, please remain calm. What may seem as a threat now are only the necessary measurements that must be taken to insure the survival of the human race. We are securing this location because it is loaded with plenty of resources for both your comfort and your needs," Ovidius said with a disarming smile. "You, who are with us, are fortunate. We have all seen the news footage and we know what's coming. They'll be here soon and although you are unaware now, we are the only ones who can save you."

An African-American male in the crowd tentatively raised his hand.

"Yes?" Ovidius acknowledged him casually.

"Are you with the government? I mean… how can you save us?" the man asked.

Others in the crowd gave murmurs of agreement with his questions.

"No, we are not with the government. We are a group willing to take the proper action on our own. The government would have you trying to vacate this area. But to where would you go?" Ovidius remained silent as he awaited a response—if any of them had one to give. When no one said anything, he continued. "Right now, people who tried to flee have found themselves stranded and unprotected. Many in Illinois are already dead and transformed. The government has no clue as to what to do, and they are taking standard precautions that have done more harm than good. Do not look for the government to help you."

"But how can you help us?" A middle-aged, Caucasian woman reiterated the other man's question.

"That is something you will learn in time. All you need to know now is that you are being helped."

Ovidius turned and walked away. Madison followed him, leaving the humans to be watched over by several other vampires.

"Are you staying here?" Madison asked him.

Ovidius shook his head. "I have other matters with which to attend, and it looks as though you have things under control here.

I have to visit the other location as well."

"All right." Madison walked outside to monitor the construction of their barricades. Some of the vampires were starting to show up with the trucks and trailers.

Ovidius followed her out before taking flight to the Target location that was closest to check on its progress.

Chapter Eight

"They still didn't answer?" Vincent asked Sarah.

"No. I'm so scared," Sarah ended the call she'd made to Linda's cell. They have been trying to reach them but with no success.

"Maybe their battery died," Vincent offered a lighter explanation rather than, "maybe they're dead".

"I'm sure that's it," Sarah agreed. It was better than thinking the worst. She was happy that her parents were still alive in California and were now safe in a government controlled safe house. Her sister was in England with her husband and children and was all too relieved to learn that Sarah was still alive. Sarah didn't bother to tell her family about Vincent's involvement concerning the zombies. She felt it was best that they didn't know.

Vincent had called his mother in Florida to see if she was someplace safe. He was so grateful she lived close to military base. He just hoped it was going to be safe enough. The thought that something he had a hand in creating could kill everyone he loved disturbed him to no end. They spoke briefly and told each other how much they loved one another before she had to hang up. Knowing his mom was still alive was enough for him right now.

They all braced themselves as the helicopter began to descend.

Vincent and the others climbed out once the helicopter landed and were immediately greeted by one of the three soldiers approaching.

"Let's get you inside," said the soldier who Vincent guessed was a Major based on the shiny gold leaf on the lapels of his jacket.

The group kept their heads ducked low as they ran towards the rooftop entrance of the state Health Department Headquarters.

Once inside, introductions were made briefly. Vincent was correct in his assumption, the soldier was a Major—Major Gregory Garrett to be exact—and the good Major didn't seem all that fond of him at the moment.

"I have strict orders from the President of the United States to assist you in any way possible so that we can put a lid on this before it gets any worse," Major Garrett said, addressing the entire group. "Unfortunately, we can't stay here for long. The rate at which people are being attacked—along the highway alone— only means it will be a matter of time before the virus and those infected reach this location. Our main objective is to get a team inside SciTech Labs and gather the information you say we critically need."

"We do," Vincent said. "And, if they're still alive, we need gather whatever test subjects we may have left in the lab. That will help."

"You didn't mention anything about 'test subjects' earlier when you told us about the files," the Major pointed out.

"Actually I did—I told them." Vincent pointed to Felicia and then made a sweeping gesture towards Samantha and William.

"And I relayed that information to our Deputy Director, Dr. Wheaton," Felicia added.

"Regardless, that information isn't in our report," Maj. Garrett said.

"I'm hoping the one ape we had that took to the test successfully is still alive. Listen, I haven't had a long time to think things out, I'm sorry. Is it going to be a problem?" Vincent asked. He tried hard to hide the anger in his voice.

"It might be, Mr. Masterson."

"Doctor, please," Vincent corrected.

Garrett paused for a moment, and then continued. "Dr. Masterson, how many subjects are we talking about and what are they? My men need to be informed and properly prepared."

"Two apes—chimpanzees to be more exact. One of them turned out to be a successful trial run. The other was sick, but not as sick as our subject zero was—the one that died and resurrected,

I mean," Vincent said.

"So, my men have to make room on the helicopter for two apes. Doctor Masterson, we'll do what we can to bring these specimens back, but if we find survivors, they'll take priority."

"I don't think you understand how important those apes are to my research. They are the priority," Vincent said.

"You would ask that I leave humans behind and take your lab animals instead?" the Major asked.

"In all honesty, Major, I don't think you're going to find any human survivors left in that building. But if your men do, I would suggest they take them only if they can fit on the helicopter along with the apes. I'll leave it at that," Vincent said. He hated having to be heartless, but it was for the greater good.

"Very well, if you say you need these apes, I'll instruct my men to bring them in. I just wanted to make sure we have an understanding. With all of the chaos erupting in several states now, we were lucky to get the team we have on such short notice. We've got the National Guard and every law enforcement agency in the state trying to keep a quarantine blockade around the infected areas. The rest are trying to get residents out of the other areas before it's too late. We've got military personnel and reinforcements flying in right now, but that's still going to take a while." Maj. Garrett said.

"So in other words, we don't have time to waste," Vincent clarified.

Maj. Garrett gave him a quick nod. "Exactly. We have people dispatched already because there's a time limit on this mission. We need you to direct the team so that they can be in and out of there as quickly as possible."

"I'll do whatever is needed to get that team back in one piece with what we'll need." Vincent's tone was as deep and commanding as he could make it. The last thing he wanted was to be so close to a cure only to discover a piece was missing from the puzzle.

"That's what I wanted to hear. Now, we have the ETA on the team. They should be arriving at SciTech Labs in less than three minutes, so follow me." Maj. Garrett led them to a room filled with monitors and other communication devices. The employees who worked there busied themselves—typing away on keyboards, or chatting on Bluetooth headsets, or both—as they tried to manage the public response.

"Here, this is our workstation we set up where you'll direct the team. They should be landing right about now." Maj. Garrett pointed to a chair in front of a desk with several computer screens on it.

Vincent sat in the chair and peered at the screens. He ignored the shaky movement from the camera and instead paid close attention to what each soldier was doing and seeing. One looked out of the window of the helicopter seeing people on rooftops waving and screaming to be rescued.

"This shit is fucked up," one of the soldiers commented as he surveyed the stranded people.

"Tell me about it," said the soldier whose camera Vincent was looking through.

"Santiago and Marks, keep your heads in the game," commanded another soldier whose ID on the screen said "Sgt. Jackson".

"Yes sir," they said in unison.

Inside the headquarters, the others had gathered behind Vincent, watching the monitors as well. They saw that down below, on the streets, more and more of the monsters were rampaging, searching for fresh victims. Through the microphones, one of the other soldiers commented that the zombies didn't seem to be attacking each other.

"Makes you wonder just how rational these fucking things really are, don't it?" Another soldier commented.

"Either that, or maybe they don't smell as good to each other as we do to them. Man, this is like some 'Night of the Living Dead' kind of shit," Cpl. Gary Marks said.

"Yeah, except 'Night of the Living Dead' was fake. This shit is real and the zombies in that movie ain't nothing like those fucking things down there," said Sgt. Jackson.

"Fuck. That was one of my favorite movies, too. I don't know if I can watch it now after all this shit right here," said another soldier off camera. The name on the screen said PFC. Wilson.

"Listen. Time to focus and get your shit in gear. We're about to land. Check your ammo. We can't kill these things, but if we shoot these fuckers in the head, they stay down for a little while. Everyone got that?" Sgt. Jackson looked around the helicopter awaiting confirmation.

"Yes, sir!" the soldiers said.

"Hell yeah," Sgt. Jackson said, slamming his clip back into his M16.

Vincent couldn't help but ponder the aspects of the soldiers' conversation. In his adrenaline fueled quest to get to safety, he hadn't really taken into account that the zombies—or whatever the hell they were—didn't attack each other upon rising from the dead. They went straight for the living and terrified.

"Team, this is Maj. William Garrett, I have Dr. Vincent Masterson with me. He's going to be directing you on this mission. I want you to keep your eyes and ears open and get in and out of there in one piece as fast as you can," Maj. Garrett said, then gestured for Vincent to take over.

"Can you hear me?" Vincent asked through the Bluetooth headset Maj. Garrett had given him. He fiddled with the headset until he felt comfortable with it attached to his ear.

"Loud and clear, you're speaking with Sgt. Jackson," one of the soldiers curtly responded.

Vincent decided to ignore his tone. He couldn't worry about everyone's opinion of him if he was going to get through this. "Okay, from what I can see, it looks like you're coming in on SciTech Labs."

"We have the blueprints downloaded, just tell us where we need to go," Sgt. Jackson said.

"When you land, our lab is on the sixth floor. Bio-engineering Level 4, room 608," Vincent said.

"Copy-that," Sgt. Jackson said.

"What about your weapons, do they have silencers?" Vincent

asked.

"Of course. We know that sound attracts these things," Sgt. Jackson assured.

"Good." Vincent took a deep breath as he gave them another prayer.

The helicopter landed on the rooftop and the team jumped out. They double timed it to the rooftop door, taking positions to cover the door and each other's backs. Vincent held his breath as he watched the progress through the soldiers' viewpoints. As a younger man, he was never interested in joining the military, but he always respected the men and women who did and the sacrifice they made. He appreciated it more now than ever before. It wasn't him going back into that hellhole; it was United States Marines braving the worst of situations. He had to take his hat off to them and at the same time, he gave a silent prayer for their survival.

The soldiers made their way inside SciTech Labs and quietly headed down the stairs to the 10th level. Sergeant Jackson gave the hand motion for the others to stop and they did. They waited as he cracked open the entrance door, taking a quick peek.

He closed the door, turning to his team. "We've got four of these things chowing down on a few dead bodies. Shit, I was hoping they'd be gone by now—or at least be on the lower levels. We're going to have to be quick about this. Every bullet's got to count. Aim for their heads."

The men in his team nodded and he turned back to the door, opening it slowly. Sgt. Nicholas Jackson took the lead, aiming the barrel of his M16 at one of the feasting zombies. The zombies looked up at the soldiers and Nicholas pulled the trigger. His bullet hit home, blowing out brain matter and shards of skull through the back of the zombie's head. His team reacted quickly, firing their weapons at the others and taking them down. Stealthily, the team made their way towards the mass of dead and undead bodies covered in gore, blood and severed body parts.

Vincent watched the live action feed and saw the gruesome and dismembered remains of dead humans the zombies were feeding on. He knew them all, fellow scientists and friends. His heart sank to his stomach as he watched the video feed. Just when he was starting to feel guilty again, something caught his eye. His eyebrows creased as he came to a realization.

Those corpses were so damaged, they stayed dead.

They were just as horribly mutilated as many of the zombies were that he'd seen so far. Eviscerated, dismembered, but not beheaded.

"Hey, I think I've discovered a connection," Vincent said, alerting the others.

"What's that?" Sgt. Jackson and Felicia asked in unison.

"Look at the dead bodies—the ones those things were feeding on. They're headless." Vincent pointed to the bodies.

"They can't survive or reanimate without their heads," Felicia concluded.

"You get that, team. Cut the heads off of those fuckers before they get back up," Maj. Garrett ordered.

"I'm already ahead of you, sir," was Sgt. Jackson's response.

He and three soldiers were already bending over the bodies of the zombies they'd shot and had taken out their knives. They began to cut through the flesh and bone as fast as they could.

"This is so fucking disturbing. Poor son of a bitch was probably someone's father or husband," one of the men commented as he completely decapitated one of the zombies.

"Better them than us. Keep quiet," Sgt. Jackson said, slicing through the last bit of skin connecting the zombie's head with his neck.

The soldiers made quick work of the zombies, tossing the heads away from the bodies. Next, they took a look at the blueprint files on their devices.

"Okay, we need to get to that end of the hallway. The main stairwell is down there. Keep your eyes and ears open," Sgt. Jackson said, leading the way. After clearing the stairwell, he lead his team down the staircase to the sixth floor entrance door and gave the hand signal, halting their advancement. Cracking open the door, he took a peak. The hand signal went up again when

Sgt. Jackson immediately spotted a body dragging itself along the floor. Its stomach had been ripped open, insides half-eaten. Its throat torn to shreds and it was missing a leg. From the bio-suit it was still wearing, Sgt. Jackson knew it was one of the scientists who worked there.

"What the fuck?" he whispered; then he looked up and down the hallway. So far, it was just the one zombie they were going to have to deal with. Motioning for his team to join him, he led them towards the zombie crawling their way.

"Oh my God, Philip," Vincent gasped. He watched through Nicholas' camera. His friend—the brilliant man that had worked diligently beside him for years had been reduced to a mindless monster.

Philip's black eyes remained steadfast on the soldiers approaching him. He crawled toward them faster. The scent of their blood filled his nostrils making his hunger rise. He could smell the heat rising off their skin and it was all he could think about—feasting on their flesh.

"For fuck's sake, put him out of his misery," Vincent pleaded softly.

"You don't think we aren't," Sgt. Jackson replied as he aimed the barrel of his gun at Philip's head and pulled the trigger. Blood, brain matter, and pieces of Phillip's skull exploded from the back of his head. He didn't stop there. Kneeling, he took his knife and removed the head, placing it beside the body.

"Shit. Do you hear that?" Cpl. Marks asked.

"Shhhhh," Sgt. Jackson said. Everyone remained silent as they listened for whatever Cpl. Marks had heard.

Down the hall, they could hear it—the sound of footsteps coming towards them, faster and faster.

"Oh shit! How many of them is it?" one of the soldiers asked, his voice wavering in fear.

"Get ready!" Sgt. Jackson said, aiming his gun.

His soldiers positioned themselves in preparation for the attack. Over a dozen zombies rounded the corner, heading towards them at top speed.

"Shit! Fall back!" Sgt. Jackson commanded, seeing that they were grossly outnumbered.

The soldiers ran back through the door heading up the stairwell. The zombies followed them, catching up with ease. They grabbed one of the soldiers, bringing him down from behind. He screamed as his gun went off, firing dozens of bullets in the air and towards the attacking zombies. Bullets ripped through the flesh of one zombie's face, tearing away skin and muscle revealing the white of his teeth through the holes in its cheek. The other soldiers turned and fired into the mob as several of them began to feast on the soldier they had caught.

"We have to leave him, let's go!" ordered Sgt. Jackson as he began to rush up the stairs.

Several zombies followed him and his men as they tried to retreat. One of the zombies reached out, grabbing a hold of another soldier's ankle, tripping him. A second zombie latched onto his shoulders as it sank its bloodied teeth into his jaw, ripping away a huge chunk of flesh. The soldier screamed wildly as he struggled to break free. More zombies climbed on top of him. Others crawled over him as they rushed to get to the remaining soldiers.

Sgt. Jackson and Cpl. Marks fired repeatedly, aiming for their heads and hitting some targets. Above them, the door swung open and five more zombies rushed at them, trapping them in the middle.

"Fuck!" Sgt. Jackson said, turning and placing his back against Marks as he tried his best to cover them.

"Jesus Christ!" Vincent said, as he watched them getting attacked. "They're going to die." He couldn't believe what he was seeing even though he knew it was real.

"Marks, it was an honor," Nicholas said, firing away, making sure every bullet counted.

"Likewise, sir," Cpl. Marks replied as he gave his all at their last stand.

"Semper Fi, bitches!" Both men yelled as their final battle cry.

Beside them, the glass window shattered, splattering them with shards that sliced their skin in places. They shielded as best they could as they moved to the side, trying to prepare for the new threat that came at them from their flank.

Cassian didn't engage the soldiers in conversation after seeing how close they were to being attacked. With his sword, he advanced on the zombies that were coming at them from the upper level, slicing his blade though their necks at a speed no human could manage. The two soldiers continued to shoot at the zombies coming at them from the lower level, trying their best to keep them at bay as the rose up the staircase.

Cassian decapitated another zombie, sending its head flying into the air. It landed on the steps next to Sgt. Jackson's feet. He kicked it towards the approaching zombies.

"A little help here!" Sgt. Jackson yelled, hoping to get the attention of their new companion.

"Who is that guy?" William asked, looking at the monitor.

"Hell if I know. He just jumped through the window from the seventh floor. Did you see the way he moved?" Vincent said as he leaned in even closer to the monitor.

"Watch your backs," Maj. Garrett told the two remaining soldiers.

Cassian turned, seeing more zombies coming into the stairwell from the lower level.

"Follow me," he said, leading them back to the seventh floor. The soldiers ran behind him carefully jumping over the decapitated corpses. They made it to the seventh level and Cassian closed the door behind them, placing his hand against it.

"You're going to need more than that to keep them back," Sgt. Jackson told him. He leaned against the door, offering his help.

"How did you know there weren't any more zombies on this floor?" Sgt. Jackson asked.

"Had there been, more would have attempted to attack you in the stairwell," Cassian said.

"We need to get to that floor," Cpl. Marks stated.

"Seems like I'm going to need more assistance than I thought," Cassian murmured as he placed his back against the door and pulled out his cell phone, making a call.

"Who is this guy?" Felicia asked out loud to no one in particular.

"Can we get a picture on him and send it in for a facial recognition?" Maj. Garrett asked one of the technicians.

"Yes, sir," a male employee said, pressing numerous buttons on his keyboard.

"Need help?" Ovidius asked upon answering Cassian's call.

"It seems I might," Cassian replied with a hint of annoyance. He never liked being wrong about anything and he never enjoyed being in a situation where he wasn't in control.

"Logan should be there shortly. I sent him to assist you against your wishes," Ovidius stated.

"Defiant as ever I remember you," Cassian said.

"Good for you that I am."

"I think I feel him approaching," Cassian said, feeling Logan's familiar aura.

"Excellent. Do you need me to join you?"

"You will be the first to know if I'm that desperate."

"Ahhh, you arrogant S-O-B. Very well," Ovidius chuckled before ending the call.

Cassian placed his cell back into his pocket. He looked at the two soldiers. "Were you bitten?"

"No," they said in unison.

"Why are you here?" Cassian inquired.

"Hold on, wait a damn minute, who the fuck are you and why are *you* here?" Sgt. Nicholas Jackson shot back.

"I don't answer to you, human," Cassian replied as he peered at them with lethal intent.

"Human? What the fuck is going on here?" Nicholas asked once again as he switched positions.

Instead of his back against the door, now he was facing Cassian with his foot against the door.

"Who are you?" Cpl. Marks asked. He stepped back, aiming his gun at Cassian.

"If you want to live one more second, I suggest you lower your weapon, human," Logan said from behind.

Both soldiers turned to see another man approaching them. The two soldiers positioned themselves so they could keep an eye on both men.

"I see you have your hands full," Logan said, giving Cassian a slight bow as a show of respect.

Back in Springfield, Vincent and the others watched in silence as they monitored the activity on the screens. They didn't know who the men were or how they got there.

"Who are these men? Get a picture of the new guy who just walked in. I want to know what the hell is going on here," Maj. Garrett ordered.

"Right away, sir," the same male technician said, trying his best to carry out the Major's demands. His fingers typed furiously over his keyboard as he sent photos of the two men to numerous government agencies.

***

Cassian's smile faded when he looked back at the two men. "Answer my question. Why are you here?"

"You answer mine," Nicholas shot back.

Logan advanced on Nicholas faster than either of the men could see him move. He wrapped his hand around his throat, lifting him into the air as he applied pressure cutting off Nicholas' air supply. Nicholas had to release his gun, as he tried desperately to free himself of Logan's grip.

"Let him go." Cpl. Gary Marks attempted to aimed his weapon to help his Sergeant, but Logan placed the tip of his sword to Gary's throat.

"Don't you *dare*," Logan made sure to add emphasis to the last word.

Gary felt the sharp tip graze the skin right over his Adam's apple. He thought it best that he lower his weapon since he was at a disadvantage.

Logan smiled. "Very good. Now I believe my friend asked you a question. This one here..." He paused to slam Nicholas against the wall eliciting a wheeze from his captive. "... He can't talk as I'm constricting his windpipe. I'll allow him to breathe once *you* give us an answer."

Gary swallowed hard, his Adam's apple visibly bobbing as it brushed against the point of the blade. Since it wasn't a top secret mission, he decided to answer. "We're here to search for any information that can help us come up with a cure. One of the scientists who are behind this is guiding us to his laboratory to gather the resources from their experiments."

"One of the scientists survived?" Cassian asked. He made sure to keep his tone even in spite of the optimism he was feeling. *There was hope yet if one of the original scientists involve was still alive.*

Cpl. Marks nodded. "Yes, sir. We're to go to his lab on the sixth floor, but we were attacked before we could get to it." He looked at his Sergeant who was beginning to turn blue in the face. "Please, let him go."

Logan smirked then released the other man. Nicholas fell to his side coughing and gagging as he gulped in air. Gary knelt beside him, checking him over.

"Let that be lesson number one, humans. You don't ask the questions. You answer them," Logan warned. "Lesson number two: You don't give the orders--"

"--You follow them," Cassian finished.

The two soldiers looked up at the two men, but remained silent. Nicholas didn't know what they were, but he wasn't completely sure they were human.

Logan smirked at the soldiers before turning to Cassian. "What are your plans?"

"My plans will most definitely include a meeting with this scientist," Cassian said. He turned his gaze on Nicholas as the solider rose to his feet.

Cassian pulled away from the door and with one hand pushed the entire door into the frame, jamming it.

"How did you do that?" Nicholas asked and was answered by a backhand from Logan.

Nicholas fell back against the wall, but managed to keep his footing. He reached for his gun.

"Think again before raising your weapon. I don't want to kill you, but I will. Besides, you were warned about asking questions," Logan reminded.

Cassian walked over to the two men, snatching the headset from Nicholas' head. "Is this how you are staying in communication with them?"

Nicholas wiped the blood from his split lip before answering. "Yes."

"What about the door, is that going to hold them off?" Gary asked. He didn't want a backhand from the tall man in front of him, but he didn't want to get eaten alive either.

"Maybe. Maybe not. I suggest we are not here to see if it will or won't." Cassian looked at the young soldier.

"We're on the seventh floor; the lab is on the sixth. How are we going to get there?" Gary asked.

"That won't be a problem," Logan answered.

"May I ask one question?" Gary presented.

"Actually, this would be your third question, but you may ask it," Cassian replied.

"Who are you?"

Cassian gave him a pointed look. "We're the only beings in the world that can help you."

The story continues in book two, "Desperate Times".

Free Preview

Read chapter one of D.N. Simmons'
Desires Unleashed
Knights of the Darkness Chronicles
Book One

Special Note:

If you love reading about vampires and shifters, then you'll love
the Knights of the Darkness Chronicles. Vampires are sexy and
bloodthirsty. Shifters are badass and powerful. On top of all that,
you ain't never going to read a series quite like this one. It doesn't
hold back. It doesn't fit into one genre. It doesn't play nice with
others, either. It marches to the beat of its own drummer. It's
intelligent, face paced and puts you right into the action.

Get ready for a brand new kind of vampire/shifter story.

Praise for the
Knights of the Darkness Chronicles:

Desires Unleashed

"In a time when vampire books have become commonplace, DN Simmons has given her readers a unique voice among the genre."
- #1 Best Selling Author GA Hauser

"A great series that should be read by any Vampire/Shifter enthusiast." **- Billy Masters**

"Once I reached my point of no return, I couldn't put this blessed book down. I finished it within five hours non-stop. That's how I roll. If I love it, I devour it."
- Bex N' Books (Book Reviewer)

"This author's work is award-winning material, and D. N. Simmons has stepped into the paranormal arena with such greats as, Christine Feehan and Sherrilyn Kenyon"
--ParaNormal Romance Review

"Simmons has written the vampire hit novel of the year! With so many middle of the road paranormal books being published, Simmons took up the torch and blazed a whole new avenue for the readers to delve into." **- Janalee Ruschhaupt - Warrior of Words.**

"D.N. Simmons delivers one spellbinding ride from start to finish in her introduction to the Knights of the Darkness Chronicles in DESIRES UNLEASHED."
– Dawns Reading Nook

The Guilty Innocent

"This was such a brilliant sequel to Desires Unleashed." - **Pure Jonel Book Reviewer**

"D.N.Simmons is fast becoming the ultimate paranormal
princess! - **A Romance Review**

"D.N. is a true literary genius!" - **Love Romances and More**

In a genre filled to the brim with vampire/paranormal novels, **The Guilty Innocent: Knights Of The Darkness Chronicles Book 2** by D. N. Simmons stands out in the crowd.- **Reviewed by Janalee.**

--A Romance Review

"Ms. Simmons has created a unique society full of vampires and shifters who are anything but ordinary, and fully realized world building that will pull readers in." **--ParaNormal Romance Review**

The Royal Flush

"This series certainly isn't losing any momentum! Usually in a longer series, book 3 is the flop where things are starting to drag or become redundant. That is NOT the case here." - **Tiffy Fit Reviews**

"D.N. Simmons has created a fantastic series, not to mention characters and the world they live in, that will be hard for readers not to become enchanted with."
--Romance Junkies

"Once again, D. N. Simmons stepped up to the paranormal plate and hit a grand slam with The Royal Flush. This author's intuitiveness to the wants and desires of the paranormal readers will leave your screaming for more before the end of this novel."
- Paranormal Romance Review

"Simmons hits the ball out of the park again."
– Pure Jonel Book Reviews

Five golden stars for The Royal Flush, however I wish I could give it five-hundred. Job well done and I think I've found my new favorite author.
Bex N' Books (Book Reviewer)

Hostile Territory

"The characters are well developed, believable, and lovable. As I said before, Darian is OMG YUMMY!! Sweet and Loving, yet, Firm and Ruthless when called for. I could go on and on cause I fell in LOVE with all of them. Thank you D.N. Simmons for bringing the Knights of Darkness to us readers to enjoy. "
--Lovetiggi's Book Reviews

"If you enjoy an engrossing series that has characters that grow with each book and storylines that literally suck you in and captivate you, then grab D.N.'s wonderful Knights of the Darkness series and get ready to be blown away by her voice as she takes you on a whirlwind ride. " **Love Romance and More**

"D.N. Simmons' supernatural world is one that I always look forward to delving more into and never fails to entertain." - **A Romance Review**

The Lion's Den

"Simmons is incredible with a pen and paper (or keys and screen, whichever works for her). This book will scare you and probably give you some nightmares, but it is worth it. The Lion's Den will be one intense read you won't soon forget."
--Offbeat Vagabond Book Reviews.

"Ms. Simmons is a talented author who is going places. I anticipate seeing her work right alongside Sherrilyn Kenyon and L. A. Banks."
–   **Love Romance and More**

THE LION'S DEN delivers a story so complex, wild and action packed, I suggest you install speed bumps to slow you down. I can attest that you may be up late reading this just to see what happens next. Ms. Simmons is a talented author who is going places. I anticipate seeing her work right alongside Sherrilyn Kenyon and L. A. Banks one of these days. If you enjoy a high octane paranormal/urban fantasy adventure, then I highly recommend Ms. Simmons Knights of the Darkness Chronicles. - **Dawn Roberto (book reviewer)**

Unholy Alliance

Nominated by Love Romance and More For: Best Book of 2012 & Best Paranormal Book of 2012!!!

Author D. N. Simmons is a writer that will thrill you, chill you and take you in directions that leaves you on the edge of your seat with her entire The Knights of Darkness Chronicles series."
- Reviewer Dawn Roberto (Dawn's Reading Nook

I TOTALLY enjoyed this paranormal series. It was sexy, it was gritty, it was horrifying, it was gory, it was heart-warming, and I think that Simmons did a fabulous job of capturing different aspects of "humanity." **- TiffyFit (Book Reviewer)**

You've seen the reviews, critics and readers alike love the
Knights of the Darkness Chronicles.

Now, here's the free preview.

Desires Unleashed

Chapter One

Detective Warren Davis shuffled through the messy
stack of files on his desk. He was searching desperately for
his drawer key. He had hidden a box of *Crunchy Crème*
glazed donuts inside and wanted to indulge selfishly in the
delicious sugary taste of, in his opinion, "*the best damn
donuts to hit the 21st century.*" Finally after turning his desk
into a disaster area, which didn't take much, he located the
key to his treasure. He glanced inconspicuously over one
shoulder then the other to make sure no one was watching.
He knew how irresistible *Crunchy Crème* could be and he
didn't want to share one morsel. He slowly turned the key
and unlocked the drawer.

There they lay, the sweets of gods. Warren didn't know
of a soul alive who could turn down a *Crunchy Crème* donut.
Slowly, he opened the box, pulling one glazed donut from
the container. He stuffed the sugary treat, in its entirety, into
his mouth, taking pleasure in the gigantic burst of sweetness
that followed.

"*Mmm, delicious ... There's got to be some smack in
these donuts to have me so addicted,*" he thought to himself
as he closed the drawer and settled back in his cushioned
leather chair. He stretched his long legs out in front of him as
he chewed the donut slowly, savoring every bite.

"What are you eating?" his partner, Detective Matthew
Eric, asked as he approached him.

He stood beside Warren's relaxing figure, noting the

huge bulges in the insides of his partner's cheeks. Matthew Eric stood six-feet-three, very muscular and extremely handsome. His physique reminded Warren of a light-weight wrestler. Matthew's skin was a perfect soft-golden shade which complemented his light-brown eyes hidden behind the mop of dark brown curls. His hand came up brushing the curls from his eyes as he studied Warren.

Warren remained silent as he swallowed, forcing one huge piece of donut down his throat then another. He was thankful for the time it gave him to think of a believable lie.

Matthew looked down at his partner, a smile spreading across his face as he watched Warren nearly choking to rid himself of the evidence. He waited patiently for the lie that would sure enough come spilling from those glaze covered lips. He thought Warren should know better than to open a box of *Crunchy Crèmes,* and think he wouldn't have to share.

"Oh," Warren managed to say, swallowing the last of his donut. "This? It's nothing." He followed up with a huge gulp of his decaffeinated coffee before smiling innocently up at his partner.

Matthew took one look at his partner's full-of-crap expression and gave him one of his own. One that said *he'd better share the goods, or else*.

"What?" Warren asked, shrugging his shoulders.

"If you don't cough it up, there's going to be repercussions," Matthew threatened playfully.

"Are you sure?" Warren asked, smiling slyly.

"Un-hmm," Matthew nodded.

"Okay." Warren began coughing and gagging playfully, attempting to bring up what he had swallowed.

Matthew grimaced. "Oh God, man stop it. You're fucking disgusting. Now, where's the damn box?"

Warren laughed as he reached into his drawer pulling out his secret stash.

"I was going to give you some anyway," he stated.

"Yeah, sure you were, ya bastard," Matthew said, unconvinced.

He all but snatched a donut from the box then sat back in his chair devouring his treat. After a few minutes, he looked at Warren.,

"Remember when we first shared a box of these donuts?"

"Yeah," Warren responded, remembering how Matthew had discovered his secret. "What made you think of that?"

"Don't know, just nostalgia, I suppose," Matthew replied.

"I remember how freaked you were that day," Warren said.

"Who could blame me? I think I got over it well enough."

"Yeah, you did."

As Matthew took another bite of his donut, he remembered their captain wanted to see the two of them in her office. Pronto. After he swallowed, he decided to inform his partner.

"Hey I forgot, the Captain wanted us in her office ASAP," Matthew said calmly, as he munched on more of the donut.

"Oh really? Nothing good can come from that," Warren said as he reached in his drawer for a third donut.

Officer Brown walked over—a tall, good looking black man, he was clean shaven, well built and the health conscious/athletic type. He wasn't the kind of person to be caught dead stuffing his mouth with calorie-laden foods. He looked down at the two detectives and shook his head in dismay.

"Hey, the Captain is looking for you two. If I was you, I'd hustle in there, on the double," he said, grimacing in disgust at the two men fattening themselves on the two-hundred-calories-per-serving donuts.

"Yeah, we know, we're going now," Matthew said,

rising from his chair.

"Damn shame," Officer Brown muttered as he walked away, leaving the two detectives to smile at each other.

They made their way to their captain's office passing a few officers who were teasing them by making throat slitting motions. Everyone suspected the captain was going to have another difficult case for the two detectives to work on. They were right.

"What took you two so long to get in here?"

Captain Michelle Lawrence asked as she sat at her desk. The two detectives noticed that they didn't get a glimpse of her long shapely legs which were hidden behind the desk. Warren suspected that she had been gawked at by one too many officers and managed to hide her assets. Her long blonde hair fell in waves past her shoulders onto her shirt front, denying them and all others a peek of her 'famous cleavage' that the majority of the male–and some female cops –admired.

"Well, you know, Detective Eric, I didn't expect to be waiting this long when I called both of you in here about five minutes ago," she said, both eyebrows raised, a finger lightly tapping the desk.

"Sorry, Captain, but Warren here, he was in the 'little boy's' room," Detective Eric fibbed quickly, not wanting to admit the real reason he postponed getting to her office, which was, he forgot.

"There's nothing 'little' about my 'boy'," Warren retorted as he tried hard to force back the chuckles threatening to erupt at any second.

Captain Lawrence looked at the two men and shook her head.

"*These two ...*" she thought to herself. Sometimes they worked her last good nerve, but she wouldn't deny that they were her two best detectives.

"Look gentlemen, it's time to get right down to business. We have a report of a body found in the alley off

79th and Cottage Grove Avenue. The preliminary report stated the body appeared to be drained of blood and the head was ... well ... missing. Furthermore, there are no witnesses. I'm assigning this case to you. It's right up your alley. Galen's on the scene already, waiting on you. Detectives Weinstein and Johnson are there right now, questioning the employee of a bakery store who discovered the body."

"Now get the hell out of here."

"Hey Captain, feel like cutting us some slack? We just got off doing the Joliet case." Warren inquired, as he glanced at the little white sheet of paper with the location of the crime scene on it. "Why not let Weinstein and Johnson handle this one?"

"Oh gee, guys," she shrugged, smiling, enjoying the moment. "I'd love to let you both sit back and eat your 'donuts' but this damn government insists I put you to work."

She shrugged her shoulders as if to ask, "*What can you do*?"

"Besides, I want my best on this one. I have another case for Johnson and Weinstein."

"As you wish," Warren commented.

He wasn't very thrilled about having to undertake another case that looked to be more challenging than the last one he just wrapped up.

"You want a vacation, take the time. Until then, it is what it is. If only they'd put more than one division per state, I wouldn't have to spread your asses so thin, but being as it is, get out there, make me proud."

"Gee, Captain, you can spread my ass thin anytime," Matthew joked, not really meaning a word he spoke.

Warren laughed, knowing the truth.

"Get out," Captain Lawrence said flatly, fighting the urge to chuckle herself.

The men gave each other a knowing look as they walked out of her office.

"Great, a body drained of blood and the head is missing. This has vampire written all over it. Damn, I'm hungry. How about later, we head over to *Calvin's* for some ribs," Warren suggested as he closed the office door behind them.

"That's fine with me. I've got the nagging feeling this case is going to be a pain in the ass," Matthew said as they grabbed their coats and headed for the parking lot.

"I'll drive," Warren said eagerly as he made a mad dash for the driver's side of Matthew's car.

"Like hell you will. You have a little too much of the speed demon in you. If you want to drag race, then do it in your own shit, not mine. Now saddle your ass into the spectator's seat," Matthew said as he pushed his partner in the direction of the passenger side of his brand new Python Triton, one of the highly desired foreign cars from Asia that everyone was buying.

It was an economy car, great on gas and it looked like a sports car. Warren admired the car and mentally noted to put the automobile on his wish list for Christmas.

"You know," Warren started as he looked around his partner's new car, "you should give this car to me as a Christmas present."

He smiled at his partner as he waited for an answer.

"Sure ... if you give me your Diamondback SUV. You know that I love that truck."

"Point taken, now, let's drop the subject," Warren said, smiling slyly.

"Yeah, not willing to give up your ride, I see." Matthew smiled broadly.

He had gotten the last word, which was hard to do with Warren. He reached for his emergency light and placed it on the top of the car, clicking on the portable siren as they sped through the morning rush hour traffic on the urban streets of Chicago.

"You know, it would be nice if the government

increased the amount of officers on the S.U.I.T." Warren said.

"That'd be the logical thing to do, but I don't think they see the practicality in it. Plus, the training is hard as hell. I barely passed myself," Matthew said, thinking back to the moments he was drafted into both the police force and the S.U.I.T.

Twelve years ago, when Matthew was twenty-one, and fresh out of college, he had joined the Police force. After being on the force for seven years, and already a seasoned detective, he was partnered up with Warren, who had been on the force for five years. They hit it off instantly and had been partners and friends ever since. They never dreamt they would become the first and only human defense against supernatural criminals.

When the supernatural race (the politically correct phrase) was exposed, the government was forced to create a nationwide policing unit to monitor and arrest certain individuals with supernatural abilities who broke the law. So they began by recruiting a hundred-thousand of the nation's top cops and military personnel who were physically fit and mentally astute enough to begin the arduous training. They worked in paramilitary tactics, and with weaponry specially designed to deal with those who possessed supernatural abilities. The training had been created to improve motor skills and heighten senses of sight, smell, and hearing, which was extremely necessary to combat and apprehend the unique criminal element in the supernatural world.

Only five hundred out of the first hundred-thousand recruited made it through the demanding process, but more were needed. The call went out for more recruits which, in the end, gave the government the additional thousand officers needed to complete the fifteen-hundred-member armed force. There was another force of two thousand civilians assigned in certain fields, specializing in forensics, chemistry, character profiling, social behaviors, and weaponry. Because of their impeccable record of being among the best of the best on the police force, Warren and Matthew were drafted by the Superintendent of Police via the Mayor of Chicago for recruitment. Due to their unique partnership and their chief's belief that it would be very beneficial to the local Supernatural Unit Investigation Team, they were reassigned as partners to the Chicago division.

"I'm glad you did pass it. I would have missed having you as a partner," Warren said.

"You and me, both. We're here. Would you look at this crowd?" Matthew said as he slowly drove closer to the scene.

The location of the crime scene was packed with onlookers. Uniformed officers worked to keep the crowd away from the scene. Cars were backed up for blocks as more and more police vehicles and media trucks pulled up. Matthew navigated his car through the helter-skelter of patrol cars, finally parking in a spot as close to the scene as he could get.

The two detectives emerged and made their way past the bevy of excited reporters and curious spectators. An ambitious reporter, desperate to get the scoop, cut in front of them as they tried to make their way to the crime scene. Before they could get one step further the reporter thrust a microphone in Warren's face and began to bombard him with questions.

"Detective! Detective! Is it true that the body is headless? Do you think a supernatural did this?" asked the blonde, female reporter in the tight blue pantsuit as she struggled to keep pace with the two detectives' long strides.

"No comment," Warren said as they approached the uniformed officer guarding the crime scene.

The answer given didn't seem to satisfy the pushy reporter as she continued to ask the same questions in a different manner.

"Detectives, are you from the S.U.I.T. precinct? If you

are, then this must have been a supernatural killing, right? What kind of supernatural did this? Was it a vampire or a shape shifter?" she asked in succession.

The two detectives ignored the line of questioning, continuing on to the yellow and black police tape blocking off the crime scene. Both men ducked under the tape in unison and continued making their way to the two detectives who were waiting for them to take over.

"Hey, Barry, look who's graced us with their presence. If it isn't the '*Dynamic Duo*'," Detective Gabriel Johnson joked to his partner Barry Weinstein who was kneeling by the body.

"Heya boys," he greeted the approaching officers.

Barry straightened himself and made his way toward his partner.

"Warren… Matthew," Barry said, giving a little 'hello' nod to the two detectives.

"Gabe and I were the first on the scene. The guy who discovered the body is over there away from the media sharks."

He pointed to a twenty-something year old black male, standing against the side of a building.

"You know how hungry the media is for a story when they get a whiff of fresh blood," he joked.

All four detectives chuckled, nodding in agreement.

"Yeah, but the guy won't be able to tell you much. He was dumping the trash that should have been dumped the night before, when he came across the body. He said, 'he saw the legs sticking out from behind the dumpster and knew something wasn't right.' That's when he called the police, who called us in. That's about it," Gabriel said.

"Captain must really like you two. She gives you guys all the coveted cases," Barry teased.

Secretly, he was upset about being removed from this case, but was trying to keep it professional. He knew his partner felt the same way.

"Yeah, remind me to send her one of those famous *Anisi* gift baskets as a 'Thank You'," Matthew retorted.

"Well, as much as we would like to stay here and chit-chat with the two of you, we've just received a call. Captain wants us. Maybe she'll bestow upon us the same generosity she's shown you two," Gabriel said.

"Ha! Don't bet on it. She wants the two of us, 'cause we're hot," Warren joked.

"Yeah, I heard she likes guys with young, firm balls," Matthew added.

"Exactly. Not old shriveled, wrinkled balls like yours, so you're both out of luck," Warren finished.

"Well, I guess I have to settle for your mother then, hey Matthew?" Gabriel shot back, smiling slyly.

"Shit, be my guest! If she has a little *Romeo* on the side, maybe she'll stop bugging me about making her a grandmother," Matthew joked, causing the four detectives to laugh.

Gabriel and Barry said their "goodbyes", wrapping up their friendly banter and began walking toward their unmarked police cruiser as Warren and Matthew headed toward the body.

Matthew and Warren looked at the sheet-covered body which lay partially behind a dumpster in alley of the *Dark Night Travel Agency*, a well-known agency that catered to the supernatural. After the supernatural race was exposed, all types of businesses saw it as another way to make a profit. This particular agency helped vampires travel during the day.

Both detectives stood over the corpse. They noted the small drops of blood spotting the sheet where the head should have been. Matthew squatted down beside the corpse, lifting the sheet to peek under. It looked to be the body of a black male and, on a closer inspection, he appeared to be middle-aged. Matthew threw a glance at Warren who seemed to be having a dilemma of his own.

Matthew noticed Warren's breathing had increased and his jaw muscles had tightened. He also saw tiny beads of sweat forming on Warren's forehead.

"Hey, keep it together, man. You don't want to attract attention to yourself," Matthew encouraged his partner in a hushed voice.

"I'll be all right. Don't worry about me," Warren said, hoping to ease his partner's concern.

Matthew returned his attention back to the corpse before him, but in the recesses of his mind, he began to think back to the time when he'd first discovered Warren's supernatural secret nearly three years ago. They'd been on a stakeout, tracking down a child molester, who would strangle his adolescent victims, dress them up as life-sized dolls, and rape their corpses.

The stakeout had gone wrong when their suspect noticed their plain, black van parked across the street from his house. Matthew and Warren had hated the idea of trying to be "inconspicuous" using the van, but they'd had no other choice. They had been sitting in the van for eight hours on the third day, their butt-cheeks had gone numb and the *Crunchy Crème* donuts they had eaten earlier had left their bellies begging for refueling. It was at that moment when the nut came bursting through the front door of his house blasting his twelve gauge shotgun at their van.

Matthew would have caught a buckshot blast straight to the head had Warren not thrown himself in front of the shot, taking the injury in his upper right shoulder. Never losing their composure, they returned fire and took down their suspect. After disarming the man and confirming his death, Matthew returned to the van to check on Warren, the partner he trusted and now owed his life to.

Warren had covered his wound with his jacket, not wanting to let Matthew see it. He insisted that it was just a flesh wound and nothing to worry about. But Matthew, ignoring Warren's protests, struggled to apply pressure to stop the bleeding. He remembered trying to snatch the jacket away from Warren who seemed to be behaving as children sometimes do, hiding their wounds from their mothers so that they won't go dabbing alcohol into the wound. He joked with Warren, in hopes to diffuse the situation and keep Warren calm by telling him not to worry, he promised it wouldn't sting. Warren however, was adamant about keeping the wound hidden until Matthew pulled at the jacket with all his might. Warren had finally relented, exposing a partially healed wound. Matthew watched in amazement as the wound continued to heal. He watched as the torn muscles began to reattach themselves. He looked on in awe and disbelief as the skin reformed over the opening the buckshot had left, leaving nothing but the blood around the area where the wound had been. He was speechless. He remembered looking to Warren for an explanation.

Matthew listened as Warren, his partner of nearly two years, confessed that he was a werewolf. Warren had decided to use the mortal terminology for his species. Shape-shifters, like himself, never used terms like 'werewolf' or 'werecheetah'. He didn't like having his secret out, knowing full well that the laws were extremely biased when it came to his kind, even if he was a cop. Even if his intentions were good, he would be fired and probably prosecuted for lying and falsifying information during exams and testing. The human race didn't trust those of the supernatural race. "Birds of a feather," he supposed. He had trusted his partner enough to give Matthew the choice of keeping his secret or revealing it. In the beginning, Matthew had felt leery about such a revelation. He wasn't sure how he felt about having a flesh-eating beast as his partner.

In the end, Matthew believed he knew his partner well enough to know that he would never eat him ... he hoped. He decided to keep the secret and their bond became even stronger. It wasn't until after Matthew knew the truth about Warren that he started to understand his strange behavior of the past; such as the constant eating of high-fat, high-protein foods. He had never seen anyone who could put away two twenty-ounce porterhouse steaks the way Warren could and this was including the side dishes. He also began to recognize the look of *bloodlust* in Warren's gray eyes whenever they went to a bloody crime scene. He wondered how the hell it slipped his radar in the first damn place. He was amazed at how well Warren could endure the strong scent and sight of blood and flesh at crime scenes. He had chalked it up to Warren's own high level of personal discipline, determination and dedication to the job.

Matthew remembered the times when Warren had broken the handle of his car door not once, but twice trying to hop out of the car in a rush. He also remembered the time they had to chase down a suspect. He had decided to cut the suspect off in the car while Warren took to chasing the perpetrator on foot. He found it amazing when Warren had beaten him to the punch and had the suspect apprehended. Now that he knew the truth, all the pieces that hadn't made sense in the past fell into place.

Now, as Matthew looked at Warren again, he could tell by the way his partner's breathing was returning to normal that he had gotten control over his *bloodlust* and hunger and was ready to get his mind on the job at hand. Matthew reached into his right breast pocket, producing a retractable metal rod that he used to further examine the corpse without actually touching the body. A uniformed officer walked over to them, giving them each a pair of latex gloves. Matthew put on his gloves without hesitation. Warren always hated wearing the gloves. The scent from the latex and the powdered substance inside the gloves always agitated the sensory glands of his nose and mouth. Nevertheless, he slowly slid his hands into the gloves.

"Hey, look at this here, come closer," Matthew said inquisitively as he gestured for his partner to take a closer look.

As both men peered into the gaping hole where the victim's head used to be, Warren's breathing began to increase, but he kept his mind focused. He looked at the broken spinal cord, the torn muscles and sinew left behind. The remaining flesh looked jagged as though the head had been ripped away from the body.

They gave each other a guarded look. The conclusion was not one they wanted to embrace, but the evidence left them with no other choice. Whatever it was they were dealing with was strong ... and vicious. That was never a good combination. So far, they had been lucky. The last case they were on had been the most grueling case since they joined the new division or rather, were "appointed" to the new division. They'd had to track down a werewolf in Joliet, Illinois.

The werewolf had run amok in the suburban neighborhoods, killing and mutilating four people. They had cornered the him on a farm right outside Joliet, after he had slaughtered two cows. The family had heard the ruckus and alerted the local police, who notified the S.U.I.T. authorities. The suspect was not willing to negotiate, so they had to take him down. At that point, Matthew had been more than happy that his partner was a supernatural. They would not have survived otherwise.

"It looks as though the fucking head was snatched off," Matthew said coming back to the present situation as he inspected more of the corpse.

He noticed that the body was fully clothed. Relief spread through his mind that if there was anything else to find, it would be Marshall Galen's job, as medical examiner, to find it. As soon as that thought came into this head, so did the dread that whatever Marshall found would just add more drama to an already dramatic case.

"Yeah, that's what it looks like. The spinal cord was snapped like a twig. The flesh of the neck is all torn at the edges. See look here," Warren pointed and made a circular motion around the neck area. "Looks a little stretched, doesn't it? Like someone or something pulled and pulled until the skin and everything in between gave way. They could have done it in a fast motion but I think ... at least I feel in my gut ... that this killer wanted to feel and savor the sensation of slowly ripping off someone's head."

Warren rose quickly, shaking his head from side to side as he walked a few paces away from the corpse.

He had to regain his composure. The thought of someone so sick and twisted that they would derive pleasure out of such a macabre act of violence disgusted him. What unnerved him most was that the remains of that violent act made him want to get down on all fours, crawl over to the headless corpse and pig out like ninety-going-north. Matthew looked at him. He knew how hard it was for Warren; he knew his secret.

"Hey, Detective Davis, you ain't gonna puke, are you?" A uniformed officer called out as he noticed Warren with his back turned toward the corpse. "Aww, don't tell me a little blood gets you two boys all green."

"Fuck you, rookie," Matthew shot back in their defense. "Don't you have some tickets to write?"

He took the gloves off, tossing them in the portable disposal unit the officer was holding. He walked to his partner, patting him on the shoulder.

"Are you okay?"

Warren nodded.

"Good. Are you ready to talk to the one lead we have?" Matthew asked.

Warren took a deep breath. He looked at Matthew and nodded. In retrospect, Warren was relieved he had confided in his partner when he did. He trusted in their relationship enough now to let it all hang out. Matthew knew his friend's "condition" even though it still shook him up, especially when Warren became glassy-eyed over spilt blood. Warren wished he had the control of the older ones; the pride of the

Pack, those who could walk into a slaughterhouse and never even blink. He marveled at the amount of self-control one must have to resist such a temptation. He admired his Pack leader, Xander, for his superior self-control. However, Alexander, known affectionately as Xander, treated his Pack with that same amount of control which sometimes got on Warren's nerves. By the same token, Xander was equally protective of the Pack; Warren respected and loved him for that.

Xander never really approved of Warren's choice to join the Police Force. He was true to the traditional ways; old traditions had wisdom. In Xander's opinion, it just wasn't wise to take up a profession that might expose your secret. Being a police officer was high on his 'hell no' list. Although, Xander did acknowledged the benefits one could gain from working within and beside the law. He wasn't blind to that fact, but he feared Warren would be exposed, then hunted down because of what he was. Xander would not stand for that. Warren remembered the heated argument he'd had with Xander when he informed him that his secret had been exposed to his partner. Xander had threatened to kill Matthew, said he knew too much, but Warren had convinced him that this exposure was a move in the right direction.

Xander had scoffed at that statement. It didn't ease his suspicions or his thoughts of killing all who knew about them. It was one thing for the whole supernatural race's existence to be exposed. It was another to announce yourself as one. Because of that, Xander kept a close eye on Warren, the orphaned son of his Pack mates.

Warren's mother and father had been murdered by a renegade group of deranged mortals. They shot both of his parents, piercing their brains with silver bullets while they were tending to their farm. Warren had barely escaped with his life. He ran into the woods, staying hidden until nightfall. Then he had gone to the one place his parents told him would be safe if anything ever went wrong. He ended up on Xander's doorstep in the middle of the night, a scared six-year-old boy. Xander had taken Warren under his wing and raised him as his own. Warren was brought up in the traditional ways of the Pack. Despite all of Xander's teachings, Warren had embraced the "mortal" lifestyle, including his career choice. Ever since his parents were murdered in front of him as a child, he had wanted to be a cop so that he could catch the bad guys.

Warren thought Xander should loosen up a bit. He knew that due to Xander's old age, change was always difficult, especially after having lived for over two centuries. His Pack Alpha was pretty much hell-bent on keeping with tradition and was most reluctant to change the old ways.

Warren was silently thankful to Xander for allowing him, however reluctantly, to work with S.U.I.T. While walking toward the one lead they had in their current case, knowing he wouldn't get much from him, Warren reminisced on the day, long past, when he had been at home watching TV and his favorite family cartoon show had been interrupted for a special news bulletin. He remembered thinking it *better be pretty fucking important to interrupt, "The Samsons"*. He'd sat there and watched history in the making as the report commenced to prove supernatural existence beyond what the human mind could comprehend. It was all over the radio and had even worked its way into the cable network channels. So even if people were watching *QueerPeople*, they were going to know the news.

Warren watched, along with billions of people worldwide, as the supernatural world was exposed for all to see, for all to know. An overambitious reporter had scooped the story of a lifetime, revealing a corrupt politician who had been bitten and turned by a tiger. He was among several other politicians who were secretly keeping an abandoned military base in Death Valley. They'd had the hidden facility specially designed to perform experiments on vampires and shape-shifters and study the results. His mouth had dropped open as he'd watched that report. He'd felt grateful that he had been skilled enough at deceiving the mortals about his true identity thus far. He had learned how to control his hungers and lust, well enough to remain unnoticed, and unchallenged (outside of Matthew).

Xander had resented everything about the outing. It angered him that shape-shifters were tortured and killed at the military base. He had known that mortals would react badly after finding out.

"Mortals always hunt down and destroy what they can't control, or understand, or what they fear," Xander had said as he made numerous phone calls to other Pack leaders arranging an emergency meeting.

Xander had been right. In the months that followed, after the humans got over the shock of supernatural beings existing in their world, mass paranoia began. People had begun to panic and there had been pure chaos. Humans started looking over their shoulders; people started killing each other over the slightest suspicion.

Warren remembered getting a call from a hysterical woman who said her husband had just shot and killed their neighbor with a sniper rifle. Her husband was convinced their neighbor was a vampire because he only saw him up and about at night. Turns out the now dead neighbor liked to take nightly walks because he suffered from insomnia. The madness didn't stop there. The crime rate increased; it was the highest in years. The ironic part of it was it wasn't the supernatural creatures that were committing the crimes, but the human race itself killing other humans as well as supernaturals.

It was not until some bills were passed a year later that the madness subsided. Angry and fed up family members were tired of fighting for their lives and the lives of their loved ones who had been turned. Those people made their voices heard loud and clear and the government had to acknowledge that the worldwide, fear-induced bloodshed had to be dealt with and fast. Martial law was enforced, giving the government time to think of a plan.

Some supernaturals, fearing they would be hunted down and slain, decided to form a Council in an attempt to gain positive exposure and establish themselves among the humans. They joined with the American government to share information and develop laws equal to those the human race already enjoyed. The human race was trying to restore order from the madness they had caused. They were trying to get control over what they could not comprehend. Many supernaturals believed that the human race was foolish and vain to think that they could be the overlords of all the supernaturals' power and wisdom. The humans had been underestimated. America was the first country to form the "Laws of Co-existence" with the supernaturals successfully. Most of Europe followed, then Canada and Asia, making the "Laws of Co-existence" partially international.

The first bill that was passed into law clearly stated supernatural creatures were now required to obey the same laws as every mortal. If they committed a murder, they were arrested and were to have their day in court. If a supernatural was suspected of a crime, and if they turned themselves in willingly, they would await their trial date for up to a period of seven days. They would then be tried by a mixed jury of humans and supernaturals (shape-shifters only), and if found innocent, they were set free but monitored ... if found guilty, they were to be executed immediately. However, if a supernatural refused to be taken into custody, they were executed on the spot. Due to their supernatural abilities, their right to "Due Process" was not equal to that of humans.

Law number two was more for vampires than shape-shifters. No drinking from mortals who were not willing. It was understood that a bite from a vampire was equivalent to sex for a human. You could not arrest and charge two adults for having consensual sex; therefore, you could not charge a vampire for getting "bloody" with someone who consented to the bloodletting. However, the union could not be fatal; it also had to be with an adult. Anyone under the tender age of eighteen was jailbait and anyone who did not consent was considered raped. In addition to this law, the willing conversion of a mortal was prohibited. It was considered suicide if a mortal consented to conversion. Of course, vampires didn't really adhere to this portion of the law.

The vampires had taken to that law rather harshly. Some of the young ones retaliated. They had no idea what humans had in store for them. If found in the act of "raping," "murdering" or "child molesting," if that supernatural couldn't be apprehended in a "peaceful" manner, they were to be shot and killed on the spot. This was stated in the news bulletin when they announced the new laws. What they didn't say was that they had gathered a great deal of information on the supernaturals, due in part to all the materials and documentation gathered from the secret facility in Death Valley. For instance, a trained mortal knew what to look for in appearance, physical attributes, etc. The government was better prepared and was well-equipped to deal with the supernaturals. The S.U.I.T. Organization was armed with ultraviolet gel ammunition for the bloodsucking undead and liquid silver-nitrate bullets for shape-shifters. These specially designed bullets would explode upon impact and work their way through the blood stream, making it virtually impossible for any to survive. Regular silver bullets hurt and took longer to heal, but didn't kill the shifter unless they struck in a vital area. Any liquid silver entering the blood stream meant an inevitable death.

Warren wondered if Xander would be able to survive a vital hit from a regular silver bullet. He suspected that because of his age he may be able to heal, if he drank the blood of the Pack Matron. However, he doubted Xander would be able to survive being shot by a liquid silver-nitrate bullet. The humans had been prepared. After a few vampires who were in violation of law number two were made examples of, the vampires were "less inclined to exhibit any *rash* behavior." Or so that's what the Secretary of State said during his speech when he announced the decrease in supernatural crime. Warren had to admit the thought of a combustible silver-nitrate bullet going through his chest *would* make *him* feel a little more law abiding. His other Pack mates had been outraged, feeling helpless against the change. Warren wondered in amazement if this was the first time the supernatural race felt truly vulnerable. He suspected Xander wasn't worried, but cautious ... always cautious.

Law number three was pretty much directed at shape-shifters. Shape-shifters were to go to a government protected and sanctioned hunting ground on the nights when there would be a full moon. Some of the Pack leaders had disputed this bill. Many said they had their own private property, and would not take too kindly to being monitored while they changed, mated and hunted. After three months of deliberation, the government relented, only to revise the bill. The revised bill now stated if one did not have a "designated" hunting ground, you were required to go to a government sanctioned one provided in each state. Once finalized, there were no exceptions to this law. If found off hunting grounds, the shape-shifter would be contained, charged, most likely deemed dangerous, then executed.

In the beginning, there were a lot of unexplained "accidents" when a supernatural was taken into custody for suspicion of committing a crime. They were often tortured or murdered by spiteful officers wanting revenge. It was during this time the supernaturals protested while their council spoke out against the cruel and illegal tactics of the government's supernatural police force. The entire S.U.I.T. organization went under investigation. The offending officers were arrested and sentenced.

The last bill to be added became law number four to

establish equal protection for supernaturals. For there were individuals and radical humanist groups who decided to turn their Thursday night poker club into outlandish cults that would chase down members of the supernatural race to destroy what they could, by maiming and killing whomever they could find. This new law, which was much needed, prohibited any type of vigilante acts of violence upon a member of the supernatural race. Many outraged groups felt that the human race should not have to share the world with "freaks". They vowed to continue their "fight against the forsaken," as they called it. Warren had arrested a few of these fanatics, satisfied to have finally rid the streets of them. Though he knew where there was one, there were several thousand. However, there were enough intelligent civilians, including politicians, who knew that to start a war with the supernaturals would incite the destruction of the human race. These individuals lobbied ceaselessly to pass law number four; they knew that the government had to offer protection to the supernaturals in order to guarantee protection for human existence.

The laws left little room for mischief and seemed to keep things under control. Supernaturals were U.S. citizens rightfully. All of humanity now knew they could not destroy the supernatural race; some humans didn't want to destroy supernaturals at all. Many historians were baffled and marveled at the whole idea of immortal creatures; beings that have seen empires rise and fall, wars begun and ended. They knew who shot two of America's most famous presidents. They knew what it was like to watch Rome burn and hear the psychotic tunes from the Emperor's fiddle. Then there was the medical scientist who wanted blood samples, urine samples, sperm and egg samples. They wanted to know what was in the supernaturals blood that was different from their own, and how to make that blood work for them.

Many other businesses including restaurants, bars,

clubs, stores, and airports opened their markets to the supernaturals. However, there were some businesses that reinstated the segregation law, barring supernaturals from "human only" establishments. Even though mankind was learning to co-exist, the two races were far from equal in all that the world had to offer. There were other bills being brought before the legislature that wanted to incorporate supernatural studies in schools as well as cultural awareness courses. This caused great debates within the ranks and the bills had yet to be voted on.

About the Author

D. N. Simmons lives in Chicago IL., with a rambunctious German Shepherd that's too big for his own good and mischievous kitten that she affectionately calls "Itty-bitty". Her hobbies include rollerblading, billiards, bowling, reading, watching television and going to the movies. She has been nominated at Love Romances and More, for "Best Book" of 2012 and "Best Paranormal Book" of 2012. She has won "Author of the Month" at Warrior of Words. She was voted "New Voice of Today" at Romance Reviews and "Rising Star" at Love Romance and More.

To learn more, and have the opportunity to speak with the author personally, please visit the official website and forum at www.dnsimmons.com . D.N. is always interesting in meeting new and wonderful people.

4294619R00115

Printed in Great Britain
by Amazon.co.uk, Ltd.,
Marston Gate.